The ~~Best~~ **Worst** Christmas Present Ever

The WORST

Best Christmas Present Ever

The ~~Best~~ *worst* Christmas Present Ever

Budge Wilson

Cover by
Tony Meers

Scholastic Canada Ltd.

To The Sisters of St. Joseph
of Peterborough

Canadian Cataloguing in Publication Data

Wilson, Budge
The best/worst Christmas present ever

ISBN 0-590-71430-9

I. Title.

PS8595.I5813W6 2000   jC813'.54   C84-098532-0
PZ7.W54Be 2000

12 11 10 9 8   Printed in Canada   0 1 2 3 4/0

Contents

1

The vase

The little fishing village was damp and chilly in the November afternoon, and in the harbour the boats rocked quietly on the cold grey water. Lorinda and James and Jessie Dauphinee stepped into MacDermid's Gift Shop, and the bell tinkled above the doorway. Outside it was snowing hard, and before long their boots started to make a dirty wet pool on the welcome mat.

Jessie, two years old last August, was holding an icicle, which began to drip down the front of her coat and onto the floor. Lorinda paid no attention. Her restless black eyes were darting around the store, feasting on the woven scarves, the bright pottery, the embroidered place mats. Christmas was less than four weeks away, and she had come to look for a gift for her mother.

Jessie's icicle had shrunk to the size of a small pencil in her wet mitten, and the welcome mat was almost afloat. Mrs. MacDermid came bustling up from where she had been helping a customer, a line between her eyebrows.

Her red hair bounced as she rushed across the room.

"Lorinda!" she cried. "Please, dear!" The dear part didn't sound all that friendly. "Must you all stand there and just drip? Shake yourselves off and either come in or go out. You're blocking the entrance."

But Lorinda scarcely heard her. She had seen it! She had seen exactly what she wanted to give her mother for Christmas. There, way over in the corner, squeezed in between the carved chess set and the box of pewter bracelets, was a perfectly heavenly red vase. It was made of pottery, and flying all over the shiny red surface were a zillion white sea gulls. Like a sleepwalker, Lorinda floated off the mat and across the room to the far table, ignoring Mrs. MacDermid and leaving Jessie with James.

"Oh, my!" breathed Lorinda, mouth and eyes wide open. "Did you ever *see* anything so beautiful?" And she picked the vase up with her slippery mittens and hugged it to her chest.

Mrs. MacDermid came running. "Lorinda!" She spoke softly, breathlessly, but with unmistakable panic in her voice. Reaching out, she snatched the vase away. "There!" she sighed. "It's safe. Now *please*, dear. Don't pick things up!"

"You don't need to be so worried, Mrs. MacDermid," snapped Lorinda, "because I'm going to buy it. For my mother. For Christmas."

All the irritation faded out of Mrs. MacDermid's eyes. "Oh, Lorinda," she sighed, for a different reason this time. "Do you know what it costs? I'm so sorry. Why don't you buy her a nice apron?"

"Because she's got lots of aprons, and anyway, aprons are work things. I want to get her a present that's just a happy thing. Like the vase. Besides, I've got five dollars all saved up from my paper route, and I want to buy her *that*." She reached out her long, thin arms.

This time it was Mrs. MacDermid who hugged the vase to her chest. But she looked sad and also kind. "Lorinda," she said gently, "the vase costs thirty-five dollars."

Way over by the door, James and Jessie had walked off the welcome mat and were moving in different directions among the display shelves and beside the tables. But Lorinda and Mrs. MacDermid didn't notice. James was peering through his glasses at all the merchandise, but Jessie was too small to see above the tables, so she just padded around the store sucking on her icicle.

Lorinda couldn't think of a single thing to say. How do you argue with a price tag? She knew that the person who had made the vase would have been paid already. The thirty-five dollars was not a price Mrs. MacDermid could change.

But Lorinda was not one to sit down and burst into tears over a big disappointment, even though she would have liked to. She held her head high and tossed her long, straight black hair over her shoulder, spraying the apron rack with loose snow as she did so. "Thank you very much, Mrs. MacDermid," she said. "I understand. I guess I can find something else that's nice.''

"Could I show you some pretty—" began Mrs. Mac-
Dermid, but Lorinda interrupted her.

"No thanks," she said, voice uneven. "I think I'll come
back and look another day." She knew that if she looked
until next August, she would never find anything else that
she wanted to buy. She knew exactly what she wanted, and
she couldn't have it, and that was that. Simple.

Suddenly, Mrs. MacDermid no longer felt soft and kindly.
"*Lorinda!*" she exclaimed. "Do something about Jessie,
and do it fast!"

Over on the west side of the store James stood at a
display counter, gazing with shining eyes at a wooden
truck. Jessie was standing beside another counter, wob-
bling on top of a cardboard carton and reaching out for a
large china figurine. Lorinda flew across the room and
snatched Jessie off the box and into her arms, just in time.

"Pretty lady," sighed Jessie, sucking on what was left of
the icicle.

"Yes," said Lorinda. "Pretty lady. But not for you."
She sighed too. "Just like the vase is not for me. C'mon,
kids. Let's go." She spoke loudly, so that James would
hear. But James was talking to Duncan MacDermid, who
had just come into the back of the shop with his sister,
Fiona.

"...and we're going to look after the store for a couple
of hours," Duncan was saying, and Fiona was nodding her
head up and down as he spoke. "Mom is going over to

Chester Basin for some stuff she needs for dinner tonight, because Coolen's Variety Store ran out of meat and lettuce.''

Duncan and Fiona both had red hair like their mother and father. "Fancy a redhead marrying a redhead," people used to say, years ago. "Why, there'll be nothing but fights and bad temper all the time in *that* house." At that point, Mr. MacDermid was new to the village so of course nobody knew him. As it turned out, he broke all the rules about red hair, because to this day no one had ever seen him angry. His red hair grew in a fringe around a shiny bald head, and he was round and short and comfortable and peaceful looking.

Mrs. MacDermid was another matter entirely. She was said to have a warm heart "at bottom," but she was prickly as a nettle, and sometimes Lorinda thought, I wonder if she'd be any more patient and cheerful if she dyed her hair black? Not that Lorinda was a very good person to be wondering any of these things. She had a pretty strong prickly streak herself, and when Lorinda and Mrs. Mac-Dermid were in the same room for very long, the sparks were almost certain to fly.

Mrs. MacDermid was already putting on her coat and preparing to leave, reminding Duncan, who was nine, where the receipt book was, how to lock the cash drawer, where to find the gift-wrap. Duncan was smart and quick moving, and he loved to make plans and tell everyone else what to do. But the gift-wrapping was Fiona's job. She was only six, but she was already what her father called a "red hot wrapper-upper." If a customer was willing to wait an extra fifteen or twenty minutes, Fiona would gift-wrap the merchandise as perfectly as any grown-up could do it. And all for free. Fiona loved having this job all to herself.

Mrs. MacDermid worried and fussed about all the paper Fiona wasted, but Mr. MacDermid would say, "Now, now, Helen. Don't worry about it. She's learning, and she's doing a good job. In a few years she'll be able to do it without wasting a single bit of paper or ribbon."

Mrs. MacDermid would place her hand over her eyes as though she had a terrible headache, and mutter, "A few *years*!" And then for a while she would make a lot of noise as she went about her business—pounding the cash register keys extra hard, slamming drawers shut, kicking the packing boxes if they were in her way.

Then she would calm down and forget all about it. She might even say to a customer who was getting a bit impatient about the length of time Fiona was taking, "You'll be *glad* you waited when you see the finished gift. Fiona does a beautiful job!" Mrs. MacDermid's temper shot up and down like a yo-yo.

Lorinda and James decided not to go home when they heard that Duncan and Fiona would be looking after the shop alone. As soon as Mrs. MacDermid was gone, they took Jessie outside so that she wouldn't break anything or get overheated; her big woolly hat was pulled down over her black curls and she had on a heavy snowsuit and thick mittens. They tied her to the fence post with a piece of strong nylon rope, leaving her enough line so that she would be able to move about a bit. She sat down in the snow happily and began making a snow pie, muttering to herself, "Jessie busy girl." From where she sat she could see the incoming fishing boats, the traffic on the road and the Millers' two hunting beagles who were barking in their pen across the road. Lorinda made sure she could watch her sister from the store window.

As soon as the four older children were alone, Lorinda told the sad story about the vase. She had already discussed it with James. "Even if James and I gave Mummy the vase between us," she said with a groan, "we'd still need twenty-eight dollars and five cents. James feels as sad about it as me. I wish like anything I was a criminal. Then I could just up and steal it. But all I can do is be miserable."

But Duncan was a born organizer. He never took the time to be miserable. "It's simple," he said, smiling cheerfully from the high stool behind the cash register. "If you haven't got the money, earn it!"

Lorinda was annoyed. "For heaven's sake, Duncan," she cried. "I'm only ten years old and I'm a girl. Girls can't help out on the Government Wharf, and Mummy won't let us do hand-lining while the boats and stages are this slippery. And I have to go to school, so I can't work in the crab factory or the Texaco restaurant. Besides, I'm too young. Just how on earth do you think I'm going to earn twenty-eight dollars and five cents? Or James. What can a seven-year-old do?'' She looked out the window and checked on Jessie, who was making snow angels and smiling to herself.

Duncan looked full of confidence, but he made no suggestions. ''Tonight we'll all think,'' he said, ''and tomorrow we'll have a meeting in your dad's barn. Then we'll all talk about our ideas and pick out the best ones.'' He fixed Lorinda and then James with his intense green eyes. ''There will be *no problem*!'' he announced.

Some of Duncan's sureness was starting to rub off on Lorinda. James had felt fine from the moment Duncan had said, ''It's simple.'' Then again, James had a way of thinking that everything was going to be fine anyway. But a disturbing thought suddenly occurred to him.

''What if someone buys the vase before we get the money?'' he asked.

Duncan paused for only a short moment. ''Still no problem,'' he said, smiling broadly, freckles bright and cheerful. ''We'll hide it!'' Everyone was silent, and a little bit shocked.

But Duncan wasted no time. Striding across the store, he took the vase, put it carefully into a brown paper bag, and opened a cupboard at the back of the office. He stuffed the bag into it, way at the back of the shelf, behind the carbon paper and the business envelopes and the stapler. Then he returned to the table where it had sat, rearranged the items on it, and started changing the locations of most of the more noticeable items throughout the store.

"I can even explain all this," he said as he swooped down on table after table and shelf after shelf. Fiona was starting to think he was looking too pleased with himself; she wished he'd ask her for maybe just one little suggestion. But he was still talking. "If Mom or Dad wonder why the shop looks different, I'll say I did it on purpose. Which I did, eh?"

"Yeah, sure," everyone replied.

"Then I'll point out," Duncan continued, "that people get bored with a store if it always looks the same. They start thinking, Why do I bother coming—they haven't got any new stuff. But if the place looks different, they think, Hey! They must be selling things fast! I'd better buy that sweater—or that cup or that scarf or that ring—right now, before someone else gets it!"

Even Fiona could see that this was pretty smart thinking. Lorinda and James looked at one another and grinned. "Maybe he's right," said Lorinda. "Maybe we really *can* do it."

"Sure," said James, nodding so hard that his black, shaggy hair flopped up and down.

"Oh gee, James," said Lorinda with a huge sigh as they started home, "wouldn't it be wonderful if we really could raise that money? All I can see right now is Mummy's face when she opens the parcel and sees that beautiful vase."

"I guess it *is* all you can see," said James, "because you just walked right past Jessie and left her tied to the gate-post."

9

"Oh my heavens!" cried Lorinda as she raced back and untied Jessie. "You're okay. Thank goodness you're okay. In fact, maybe—just maybe—everything is going to be okay."

But as she turned toward home, there was a worried frown between her eyebrows.

2

Reginald

The snow had stopped and the sun was setting behind Mrs. Murphy's Hill as Lorinda and James and Jessie walked home. The sky was ablaze with a winter sunset, and the afterglow touched the snow with shades of rose and warm orange. Jessie stopped in her tracks and pointed to Mr. Hyson's Hill. "Look!" she cried. "Snow pink!"

"Yes," replied Lorinda. "It *is* pink, but if we don't get moving it's going to be black pretty soon. C'mon. I told Mummy we'd be home long before dark."

But just then George and Glynis Himmelman came around the bend beside Corkum's fish store, and they all climbed over the snowbanks and down the slippery rocks to the little beach beside the Government Wharf.

Glynis and George both had blond hair and eyes the colour of blueberries. Glynis was five, with long pigtails and a turned-up nose, and cheeks that were always pink.

George was the kind of person who seemed to know everything. He was only nine, but he knew the names of stars, where to find lady's-slippers in the spring, how steam engines worked, the difference between Liberals and Conservatives and NDPs, where the trout ran and how to tie knots that didn't come undone. Even when he didn't know something, he thought he did.

"What are you giving your mum for Christmas?" Lorinda asked George, who was one of her best friends. She hoped that he would say something like, "Oh, I dunno yet," or "Gee whiz, I haven't got enough money saved up for it yet," or even "An apron," because Lorinda still didn't think that an apron was a good enough present for a mother.

But George said, "I got her a really pretty gold chain that she's been looking at all fall in Murphy's in Halifax."

"*Real* gold?" exclaimed Lorinda. "I just bet it isn't!"

"Well, no, not exactly," muttered George. "But she really wanted it badly, and it's very expensive. I've been helping Dad with his filing the past three weekends, and I'm awfully rich."

Lorinda stiffened her jaw. Awfully rich! If you really were awfully rich, you shouldn't talk about it. At least, not to someone who needed twenty-eight dollars and five cents for a red vase with sea gulls all over it. "Huh," she answered, feeling she should say something, but not wanting to say anything especially nice.

"And I got a really neat silver pen for my dad," added George.

"*Really* silver?" asked Lorinda, knowing she shouldn't.

"Oh, for gosh sakes, Lorinda," groaned George. "Why do you have to keep asking that? It's silver coloured. It's nice. He'll like it. So who cares if it's real? It cost a whole lot."

"Oh, money, money, money!" snapped Lorinda. "I knit my dad a big long red scarf and some mitts for when he's out lobstering, and he's going to *love* them, and they didn't cost a million dollars! It took hours and hours of hard work, and that's the very best kind of present. Who cares about all that old money!"

"For Pete's sake, Lorinda!" cried George. He kicked a huge clam shell, but it was frozen hard into the sand, and he stubbed his toe. He grabbed his foot and jumped up and down on one leg. "Why do you have to be so mad? What are you giving your mother?"

Lorinda held her head high. She crossed her fingers and whispered, so that Jessie wouldn't hear, "A gorgeous red vase from MacDermid's store, and James and I are going to earn the money to buy it." Her voice lost its sharp edge. "Somehow or other," she added sadly, and two big wet tears rolled down her cheek. Even in the growing darkness George was embarrassed to see them slide down her face and plop onto her coat collar. He knew it was okay to cry if you had a truly good reason, but Lorinda almost never cried. She was so tall and so tough and so strong. Sometimes she was so fierce that she almost scared George, and George didn't scare easily. He didn't know what to say. Lorinda *crying*!

Suddenly a figure jumped out from the shadow of an enormous rock, shrieking, "Grrowwwwwwwwweeeeek!" Then the scream changed to ugly laughter. Jessie rushed over to hug Lorinda's knee, sobbing into her leg. Whoever it was had a ski mask over his face, and his laugh was wicked and horrible.

Then he snatched off the mask, and there were Reginald Corkum's small, beady eyes peering at Lorinda's face. He had quite a handsome face, but his expression was so disagreeable that his nose and mouth and chin and cheeks didn't have a chance to be anything but nasty.

"Crybaby!" he yelled. "Lorinda Dauphinee's a big, fat crybaby!" Lorinda put her mittens over Jessie's ears so that she wouldn't be able to hear any of the things that Reginald might say.

"And you'll never never make enough money to buy your mother a Christmas present," he went on. "Everyone knows that the Dauphinees are poor. How come every other fisherman in the village makes lots of money, but your dad can't seem to catch enough fish to even pay the grocery bill? So *there*!" He stopped speaking, folded his arms across his chest, lifted his chin, and smiled a horrid smile.

Lorinda knew about that grocery bill. So, apparently, did everyone else. She wasn't sad anymore. She was so mad she felt as though her eyes were going to pop right out of her head. She reached out and caught Reginald by the collar and held him fast. With the other hand she patted Jessie's

14

head, while James wiped off her dripping nose and got her to keep her fingers in her ears. If Jessie found out about that vase, she might tell everyone in the whole village.

"Listen here, Reginald Miserable Corkum," Lorinda started, speaking through clenched teeth, "you with the big mouth and the cold icy heart." She paused for breath. "How *dare* you scare my little sister! How dare you call me a crybaby! And a big *fat* crybaby at that! I could beat you into mushed up porridge with both my hands tied behind my back. I could stomp on your head until all your brains flew out your ears!"

She let go of his collar and pointed at him with her wet mitten, fixing him with her fiercest and most terrible look. "And you're wrong, Reginald Miserable Corkum. My father happens to be the very best fisherman in this harbour, but he has weak lungs and is sick a whole lot. And being poor doesn't happen to be the worst thing in the whole entire world. And what's more, I *will* earn that money for that Christmas present, and your mother will be so jealous when she sees it that she won't sleep at night for a month and a half. So *there* to you too! Now *scram!*"

Reginald raced off in the direction of his house. Once he was over the rocks and out of reach of Lorinda's long arm, he turned around and yelled, "Nya! Nya! Nya! Dummy Dauphinee! *Poor* Dauphinee!"

"Gee whiz, Lorinda," sighed James. "Reginald Corkum has been mad at you ever since you didn't ask him to your ninth birthday party. Remember that day? He just sat outside the house behind the woodshed looking sad. Mummy kept begging you to invite him in.''

"Yes," said Lorinda. "And I wouldn't. Because the year before, he stuck pins in all the balloons and kept pulling the kitten's tail and shrieking. I wasn't going to let him spoil another party.''

George nodded. "And then he was furious when we had that spelling contest in school and you didn't pick him to be on your team.''

Lorinda shrugged. "Well, he can't *spell*. What could he expect?''

"Yeah, I know," said James. "But it must be really awful to be dumb. Especially when his dad is rich and smart and expects him to get good marks, and gets in a rage when he doesn't. It's not like he has brothers or sisters to stand up for him.'' James sighed again. "It must be terrible to be Reginald Corkum," he said, "but he sure makes it hard for people to like him.''

"You can say *that* again," retorted Lorinda. "If he wants to have some friends, he should just start being nice for a change. He might get quite a surprise.''

Lorinda wasn't mad at George anymore. He might be a Himmelman, and heaven knows the Himmelmans had lots of money, what with their father being a lawyer and all, but at least he wasn't Reginald Corkum, and he was a friend. She sat down on a large, icy rock in the pitch dark, and told George and Glynis the whole story, while James took Jessie down to the end of the beach to look for periwinkles. The stars came out and the moon shone down on the slippery sand, and everyone stomped their feet up and down to keep warm.

When Lorinda had finished her tale, Glynis was feeling so sad for Lorinda and James that she was groaning out loud, but George raised his arm for silence.

"We'll *all* go to that meeting in your barn tomorrow. There are six heads among us. . . ." He paused and looked down the beach at Jessie. "Six and a half," he corrected. "And I know—I *know*—we can figure out a way to fix up your problem. Your mother"—he paused dramatically and raised both hands like a preacher—"*will have that vase!*"

Lorinda felt her whole heart melting into a big buttery pool. You can't hug a boy when you're ten, but she certainly felt like hugging George. But then she suddenly had a terrible thought.

"Oh my heavens!" she cried, peering at her watch by the light from the Government Wharf. "It's half-past-six! Mummy will be so sure we're all drowned or run over or kidnapped that she'll have twenty-five million fits."

She yelled for James and Jessie to come and to come fast. Then she scooped up Jessie, gave her a big hug, and raced off in the direction of home. James slithered over the ice and did his best to keep up with her. He fell six times before they reached the Dauphinee house.

3

Making plans

When Lorinda woke up next morning she let her mind slide over and off the events of the night before. They had arrived home an hour and a half late, and Mrs. Dauphinee had been frantic, particularly because Mr. Dauphinee was sick in bed with bronchitis again and she didn't want to worry him. And he got out of bed three times to ask if the children were home yet.

Lorinda had been right. Her mother had been sure that all three of her children were at the bottom of the sea, or ground to a pulp by some transport truck, or taken off to Vancouver by a masked man in a big car. At six-thirty, when she finally saw them from the window, panting and guilty-looking and perfectly well, her first feelings were of enormous relief. As she watched them racing up the road past Mr. Hyson's house she whispered, "Thank you. Oh, thank you, thank you," and blew her nose, clearing her throat in order to get the frog out of it.

But by the time they actually entered the kitchen she

could hear Mr. Dauphinee coughing and coughing in the bedroom, and she was so cross she could hardly speak. And Mrs. Dauphinee wasn't an angry kind of person. All she seemed to be able to say was, "How could you *do* this to us?" and all Lorinda and James could think of to say was, "We're real sorry, Mummy."

But by bedtime, all that frozen fury had melted out of her soft brown eyes. She had sat down on Lorinda's bed and told them a story, just as she did every night of the year. She made them all up, and every single one was different.

Before she said good night she told them, "I'm sorry I was so angry. It's just that I was scared to death, and there seem to be a lot of things to worry about these days." Then Mr. Dauphinee came out of his bedroom (this was strictly forbidden) and went into their rooms to give them special good-night hugs.

But now it was another day, and it was bright and sunny and crisp and cold. Lorinda rose and dressed quickly, and then went in to wake James. He rubbed his eyes and then flopped over on his stomach and went to sleep again.

"James!" said Lorinda sternly. "Today's the day. The meeting. We get to figure out how to earn the money for the vase, so get a move on! *Wake up!*" She shook his shoulder.

James staggered out of bed with his eyes shut tight, and padded off to the bathroom. He couldn't see much anyway without his glasses. Lorinda raced downstairs and started pouring juice and making toast. Jessie was already up and dressed, and was pushing her doll carriage around the kitchen at top speed. Mrs. Dauphinee came in from their father's room carrying a tray, and gave Lorinda a big kiss on the top of her head.

"Morning, sweetheart," she said. "What's on for today? It's a beautiful day for a Saturday."

Lorinda was careful about how she answered. "Well, uh..." she began, "George and Glynis and Fiona and Duncan are going to play with us in the barn. Petunia won't mind, being the only cow in there and all. We'll probably be up in the loft anyway. Can you keep Jessie in here?"

"Yes, I can, and no, I'm sure Petunia won't mind; but why on earth do you want to spend the day in the barn when you could be outside coasting?" Mrs. Dauphinee put Mr. Dauphinee's breakfast dishes in the sink. "Mind you don't fall out of the loft," she added. "I don't feel like being terrified out of my wits again before twenty-four hours are up. The eggs are in the pot on the stove. Better have one. And give one to James, too, when he comes down, please. Thanks." Then she rushed off to take Mr. Dauphinee his coffee, humming "Jingle Bells" to herself as she went.

Later, after James and Lorinda had kissed their father hello and goodbye, and put on their outside clothes, they went out to the barn. George and Glynis were already there, talking to Petunia and feeding her hay.

"I wish we had a cow," said Glynis.

"You've got two cars," said Lorinda, somewhat snappishly. "You don't need a cow."

Glynis couldn't see what cars had to do with cows, but she kept her thoughts to herself. She just said, "You can't talk to cars. Or feed them hay. I just love Petunia. You can't love a car."

Lorinda thought about that. It seemed to her that she could come pretty close to loving a car. All the Dauphinees had was a truck, and although it was a nice truck, it always seemed to be full of salt fish. If all five Dauphinees wanted to go somewhere, two or three of them had to crawl in back with the fish. No, Lorinda thought, it would not be hard to love a car. But they had not come out here to discuss cars and cows.

"Well," she said, sitting down very straight on the milking stool and folding her hands in her lap, "how are James and me going to earn twenty-eight dollars and five cents before December twenty-fourth?"

"We've each got a good idea," said George. "You go first, Glynis."

Glynis knew that George was letting her go first because he thought his own plan was better than hers, and he wanted to save his until last, like the frosting on a cake. But though she was only five years old, she felt her ideas were every bit as good as his. "You can make things to sell in MacDermid's Gift Shop," she said. "Shell ashtrays and pebble men and aprons and sock animals and hasty notes and things."

Lorinda scratched her head. "Our sewing machine is broken," she said slowly, "but I'm a pretty good artist. I bet I could make some really nice hasty notes. Scratch pads are cheap, and we could put them in Mummy's plastic wrap." She gave Glynis a little pat. "Good idea, Glynis."

"And now," said George, "*my* idea! You can set up a refreshment counter at MacDermid's too. People sometimes stay in there so long they must get awfully hungry. You could lug over a card table and have a lemonade stand. Soda crackers would be fine for food, and there are about a million in a package. I bet you'd make a fortune!"

Lorinda was pleased. It was only ten in the morning and they had two good ideas already. And James could help with both of them—wrapping notes, pouring lemonade, taking in the money. Already she was starting to feel better. "We'll just show that Reginald Corkum," she muttered. "Bet you anything he gives his mother an apron."

Just then Fiona and Duncan arrived, out of breath, freckles shining in the morning sun. Fiona could hardly wait to talk about their ideas.

"Hey, James!" she yelled, because James was almost exactly her age and one of her special friends. "I've got a great plan for you to make money. Just look around the harbour. Dirty cars all over the place. Daddy says the salt uglies up the outside of the cars and wrecks them underneath in the winter. How about you starting a car-wash business?"

James grinned broadly. His eyes shone behind his glasses, and he forgot how cold it was in the barn.

"Oh, Fiona," he gasped. "That's a great idea. I can get

a bucket and some cleaner and some rags, and if there's a thaw I can even use the hose. I'll make every car in this village so shiny it'll look brand new. And," he grinned again, "in two days they'll all be dirty and have to be washed all over again. Oh, Petunia!" he said, giving the cow's kind face a hug. "I think we're going to be rich in no time at all!"

James didn't usually get so excited. He would get very pleased, but not really steamed up, so he must have thought that the car-wash idea was a truly marvellous one.

It was hard for Duncan to wait all this time in silence. He was slapping his hands together to keep them warm, but mostly just to keep busy. "My idea," he broke in, "is that Lorinda gets to be the Himmelmans' cook and baby-sitter on Friday afternoons and Saturday mornings. Mrs. Himmelman goes into Halifax late every Friday afternoon, and again on Saturday to do her Christmas shopping and to visit her old Aunt Hattie in the hospital. Well, Lorinda's a good cook and a really great baby-sitter. She can get lunches or suppers for the Himmelmans when their mum goes away. Then Mrs. Himmelman won't have to get the meal ready before she leaves, and Mr. Himmelman won't have to get it when he arrives home tired from work, and George won't have to make macaroni and cheese and James can play with Glynis so Mr. Himmelman won't be disturbed while he's reading *The Mail Star*." He panted a little after his long speech and then went on. "The whole family will be really pleased," he concluded.

"Hi!" said a small voice.

Everyone swung around, but there was no one there.

"Jessie!" exclaimed Lorinda. "In the loft! And alone!" She was already halfway up the ladder. She was right. There was Jessie, clad only in a sweater and jeans, sitting in the hayloft with her feet dangling over the edge. James was so terrified that he managed to cram all his fingers into his mouth, and his eyes almost jumped out through his glasses. He didn't dare speak. When Lorinda was close to Jessie she stopped rushing.

"Nice Jessie," she said softly. "Dear old Jessie. Don't move. Don't move one muscle." At last she was there, grabbing Jessie by the arm and hauling her down to a safer level. Everyone below started to breathe again. But not for long.

"What if she heard everything?" said James, thinking about how careful they'd been yesterday to keep her from hearing.

"Oh, glory be!" gasped Lorinda. "She probably heard every single thing. Look, Jessie," she pleaded as she wrapped an old blanket around her sister to keep her warm, "don't tell Mummy about the vase. Don't tell Mummy about our plans." Then Lorinda clenched her fists and stared at the barn rafters. "Oh, for Pete's sake! I'm never sure if she understands what I say. She says so little."

"Nice vase," said Jessie. "Red."

"So little," said George, "but too much."

"Oh, Jessie!" begged Lorinda, stooping down and taking Jessie's shoulders in her hands and staring into her large, violet eyes. "Don't *say* that! Never say 'nice vase' again. It's a secret. *A secret!* Don't tell!"

Jessie shook her black curls vigorously. "Secret," she said solemnly.

But there was no time for more. Suddenly Mrs. Dauphinee dashed through the barn door, apron flying, a mixing spoon in one hand and a dishcloth in the other. "Jessie!" she was yelling.

"It's okay, Mummy," called James. "She's here." Lorinda handed the blanket full of Jessie over to her mother.

Mrs. Dauphinee hugged her close and closed her eyes. "I'm not sure I could survive any more shocks for at least a week. Last night, that awful wait; this morning, Jessie. I guess she heard you say you were going to the barn, and she just took off when I left the door open after I burnt the toast. All my fault. Oh, Jessie! I'm so glad you're all right."

When Mrs. Dauphinee had disappeared with Jessie, Lorinda sank down on the milking stool. "Well," she sighed, "Jessie may be okay, but I'm not. I probably won't sleep a single wink till Christmas Day. Even if we do raise the money, I'll be holding my breath for four straight weeks, wondering if Jessie is going to spill the beans. Oh, brother!"

But Lorinda was never one to brood for long. She stood up. "I would like to thank the members of the committee for thinking up so many good ideas." She blew on her cold fingers. "Now, as it seems to be warm outside and cold inside, I think the committee members should pick up their toboggans and go over to Hyson's Hill to do some coasting. I move," she said, bowing slightly, "that the meeting be adjourned."

For the rest of the morning they had a beautiful time tobogganing. In the afternoon Lorinda and James went off to Coolen's Variety Store and bought lemonade mix and paper cups and a giant box of soda crackers.

"We'll get the salty kind," said Lorinda, "because they make you thirsty." This took up a lot of Lorinda's five dollars and most of James' dollar ninety-five, but they were both pleased all the same.

They were so excited at supper time that Mrs. Dauphinee had to keep reminding James to eat his pancakes, even though he loved pancakes and was really hungry. Lorinda got the giggles and choked on her applesauce. All the fun rubbed off on Jessie, who paraded around the dining room singing songs off-key and smashing her cymbals together.

"They're all crazy," said Mrs. Dauphinee to Mr. Dauphinee, who had chosen a noisy supper for his first meal out of bed. "But nice," she added.

"And a whole lot nicer," grinned Mr. Dauphinee, "than staring at the four walls of the bedroom."

"She doesn't know how nice!" whispered Lorinda to James. That night she had dream after dream in which Mrs. Dauphinee was unwrapping the red vase. But in one of the dreams, the vase broke as it was taken out of the box, and in another it was Christmas morning and Lorinda couldn't find it. She and James looked all over the house frantically and in a terrible rush, but it was nowhere to be found. So when Lorinda woke up, she was only half sure that everything was going to be all right. She felt even less sure when Jessie appeared beside her bed.

"Secret!" whispered Jessie, with her fingers on her lips. Then she squealed, "Red vase!" and yelped with laughter. Nobody heard her except Lorinda, but all the same, she could feel her heart beating right through her ribs, and her nerves felt like a collection of jumping beans.

4

Plan number one

"And what in heaven's name is all *that*?" Mrs. MacDermid was standing at the door of her store, hands on her hips, her face flushed. On the door stoop stood Lorinda and James, carrying a card table between them and staggering under the weight of shopping bags bulging with pitchers and glasses and boxes and a huge red-checked tablecloth.

"You don't actually plan to bring all that stuff into our shop, do you?" continued Mrs. MacDermid. "And what on earth is it all for?"

Lorinda was so amazed that she didn't even feel angry. James felt like running, as fast as he could, all the way to Halifax.

"Didn't they *tell* you?" gasped Lorinda, her face pale and worried.

"Didn't who tell me what?" asked Mrs. MacDermid.

"Oh, James!" groaned Lorinda, and set down her packages. "You might just as well put down the table and rest. You'll need your energy for carrying it all back home."

Now, when Mrs. MacDermid was faced with a furious Lorinda or a careless Lorinda or a naughty Lorinda, she could become as angry as her red hair allowed. But Mrs. MacDermid had a kind heart under all her fire, and when presented with a sad Lorinda, she could feel as much sympathy as the next one.

"Wipe your feet off, you two," she said, "and come inside. Someone has a lot of explaining to do. And mind you don't drip all over everything." It was one of those dismal Nova Scotia days when a sudden thaw can make a November snowfall into a mixture of rivers and slush. The weatherman described such a condition as "intermittent drizzle."

"Duncan!" called Mrs. MacDermid. "Fiona! Come here! And quickly!"

When Duncan and Fiona appeared they were greeted by two wet and woebegone figures standing on the welcome mat, surrounded by the table and the bags. Duncan clapped his hand to his forehead. "Great jumping grasshoppers!" he wailed. "We forgot to tell Mummy!"

Fiona rushed over to her mother and yanked her skirt. "Please, Mummy," she begged, "don't be mad. It's such a good idea. Just listen."

And then Duncan told all about how the Himmelmans and MacDermids and Dauphinees had met in the barn yesterday to figure out ways for Lorinda and James to make money to buy their mother's Christmas present. He explained to his mother that he and Fiona had agreed with

George that it was a marvellous idea to serve lemonade and crackers to the MacDermid customers.

"Yes," said Mrs. MacDermid, heart heavy, "a truly marvellous idea. An idea one would have liked to hear about in advance, of course, but a marvellous idea." This was even worse than she had feared. Her imagination conjured up visions of cracker crumbs from one side of the store to the other, of customers spilling lemonade all over the merchandise, of noise and confusion all day long. But she was, as she later explained to her husband, "painted into a corner." She couldn't say no at this late date without looking like a terrible villain.

"Duncan," she sighed, "you and Fiona move that display table out of the corner and into the centre of the floor." Where everyone will fall over it, she thought to herself. "And the Dauphinees can put their card table in the corner. I'll give you a couple of buckets of water so you won't have to keep trailing back and forth through the store to the kitchen. Please"—she sighed again—"try not to make too much racket, and if it's humanly possible, don't spill anything."

Although it was just nine-thirty in the morning, customers were already starting to arrive. The shop was not big, and there was a lot of bumping and lurching and jostling and excuse me's before the display table was moved and the Dauphinee lemonade stand was set up.

It seemed as though the day was going to be a huge success for James and Lorinda. The first customers were charmed by the refreshment centre with its two young clerks, and cheerfully bought the watered-down lemonade and munched on the dry crackers. In fact, the group around the table was so eager and eventually so large that Mrs. MacDermid started to wonder when they'd stop being thrilled by the lemonade stand and start being thrilled by the shop merchandise.

However, by ten-thirty the store was starting to be crowded, and the customers moved about the shop, carrying their paper cups and, as Mrs. MacDermid had feared, scattering cracker crumbs far and wide. As Lorinda and James made more and more money (two dollars and fifty-five cents already!) they became less nervous and more excited, and less careful and more noisy.

It was while Lorinda and James were serving an over-full glass to a fat woman in a mink coat, that Reginald Corkum entered the store. He walked right up to the Dauphinee table (without wiping his feet) and gave the fat lady a big push so he could get close to the lemonade. Down went the yellow lemonade over the front of the mink coat, and the lady was furious. Mrs. MacDermid, of course, had to rush out to the kitchen and bring clean wet cloths to mop up the woman's coat, and then the angry customer flounced out of the store without buying a single thing.

"Now you've fixed it!" cried Lorinda, wanting to throw a whole pitcher of lemonade at Reginald.

"I know," agreed Reginald with a smug grin, carefully dropping one of his dirty wet mittens into one of the buckets beneath the table.

"Oh, gee! Sorry!" he cried. "I guess I dropped my mitt." Then he plunged his hand into the bucket to get it, and wrung it out, mud and all, right over the bucket.

"Get out!" shouted Lorinda as she carted the pail of dirty water across the store to the kitchen. Most of the customers stopped in their tracks and wondered who Lorinda meant. Mrs. MacDermid put her hand over her eyes and counted to twenty-five. A cross customer snapped at her, "Well! Are you going to wait on me, or are you going to just stand there all morning with your eyes closed? And who is that creature who just slopped water all over my feet?" Mrs. MacDermid pulled herself together, made suitable apologies, smiled tensely, and tried without success to interest the woman in an expensive set of place mats.

In the meantime Reginald Corkum, all cheerfulness and politeness, told Fiona that he liked her pink sweater. Fiona was pleased. Maybe Reginald was an okay person after all. Perhaps James was right when he said that Reginald was only mean because no one was nice to him. "Gee," said Reginald, "I sure would like to see the present that Lorinda and James want to buy for their mother. It must be really swell."

"Well..." Fiona hesitated. "It's supposed to be a secret, but if you promise not to tell, I'll show it to you for one second," and she took him into the office and pulled the bag out of the hiding place. Reginald took one short, hard look at the vase, and then he said, "Thanks." As he left the office, he turned around and chanted,

"Know a secret. Let it out.

That's the way to be a goat!"

Then he walked straight over to Lorinda and James and announced, "I just saw your mother's present. I wouldn't even buy that for a spittoon. It's so ugly that your mother will probably cry on Christmas morning and all afternoon."

Lorinda was so mad she was both purple and speechless, and even James, who usually was able to see two sides of everything, shook with anger. "Reginald Corkum," he hissed, "you take your mean old mouth and take it home with you. Or *else!*"

"Or else *what*, pipsqueak?" asked Reginald sweetly, towering almost a head over James. Then he sauntered about the store looking at the articles on the tables, stopping to make a face at James, spilling cracker crumbs on the floor and on the counters. As he sipped his lemonade he kept saying, "Yuck! Awful stuff!" Soon Lorinda and James found that fewer and fewer customers were coming to them for drinks.

Mrs. MacDermid, who had seen enough spilt lemonade and swept up enough cracker crumbs for one day, discovered that she had a splitting headache. "Give me half an hour," she said to Duncan, "and I'll be back. One aspirin and a quick nap, and I'll probably be all right. And Duncan, I'm really sorry, but we can't have another day like this. Even if they have to set up their lemonade stand on the

Government Wharf in a blizzard, it can't be in here."

"Aw, Mum," complained Duncan, "why?"

"Listen, Duncan," she said, rubbing her temples with both her index fingers, "we've already lost a lot of customers because they couldn't stand the noise and the mess. And this is the way we make our money—for clothes, for food, for everything. Lemonade has been spilt on so many things that I'll have to spend all evening washing and ironing some of the aprons and place mats, not to mention our display covers. And it will take a good hour's work just vacuuming the store to clear up the cracker crumbs from the floor. I know that you and Fiona and the Dauphinees will help, but it all just makes my life too complicated at a time of year that's too busy anyhow. You'll have to tell them."

Duncan's heart felt like a hard, heavy knot as he tried to figure out a way to give Lorinda and James the sad news. But the next half hour was too busy for him to be able to speak to them, and he actually made two sales in his mother's absence.

When she returned, she looked more rested and a lot more cheerful. "It's okay, Duncan," she said. "I'll tell the Dauphinees. Don't worry—I'll be nice about it," and she went over and bought a glass of lemonade to drink while she talked.

She explained about the lost customers and the spilling and the racket and the clutter, and then she said, "Lorinda and James, I'm truly sorry. But you'll have to find another way to make money. This store is just too small to have all these things going on at the same time. There must be another way to earn money to buy that vase," and she looked over at the corner where the vase used to be kept.

Mrs. MacDermid spoke very quietly. "Where is the vase?" she asked. "Did someone buy it?"

No one answered. Her voice lost its softness. "Duncan! Lorinda! *Where is that vase?*"

Reginald Corkum jumped out from behind the Micmac baskets. "*I* saw where the vase is!" he announced, "if anyone would like to know!"

"Well, I for one would like to know!" snapped Mrs. Mac-Dermid, her temper rising. She was thinking of how many groceries could be bought with that thirty-five dollars.

"It's in a brown paper bag at the back of the second shelf in the office. Put away. Hidden. Where none of your rich customers have a chance to see it or buy it. Where you can't make any money off it." Reginald smirked openly at Lorinda.

For the next fifteen minutes there was enough fury in the shop to scare away any customers who might have been brave enough to stay around that morning.

Duncan was cross at Fiona for telling Reginald about the vase. "How *could* you?" he snapped at her. Mrs. Mac-Dermid was angry at Duncan for hiding it in the office. "You had no *right*!" she cried. All the children were furious at Reginald, who left the store whistling a Christmas carol—a Christmas carol!—about peace on earth and good will toward men.

Lorinda felt as though she were mad at the whole

world—at her father for being sick and poor, at her mother for needing a beautiful present, at James because he wasn't as mad as she was, at Mrs. MacDermid because *she* was so furious, at Duncan and Fiona for letting her get into this mess, and at George Himmelman for thinking up such a dumb idea in the first place. "Dumb! Dumb! Dumb!" she kept muttering under her breath. She was also angry at herself for losing her temper, for choosing crumby crackers to serve, for thinking she could make a fortune selling lemonade in an overcrowded store in the middle of winter. Most of all she was blazing, raging mad at Reginald Corkum for being the most infuriating person she had ever known.

Suddenly Lorinda knew that she had to get out of the store before she started throwing things or screaming or kicking over the water buckets. She glared at Mrs. Mac-Dermid and Fiona and Duncan. Then, with great dignity and her fiercest of looks, she said in a loud, raspy voice, "So sorry to be a bother!" and grabbed her coat and boots and stalked out of the store and slammed the door. Then she opened it again, picked up the door mat on which was written *Welcome*, and turned it over on its face before she went out and slammed the door again.

Although he was only seven, James knew they shouldn't leave the MacDermid store with all that mess to clear up. But he didn't know what to do about all the confused bitterness that surrounded him, so he just walked out from behind the card table, fixed his eyes on the floor, and put on his boots and coat. Then he turned to Mrs. MacDermid and said, "I'm sorry it wasn't a very nice day."

When the door closed behind him Mrs. MacDermid looked around the store, which had been neat and tidy and beautiful three hours earlier.

"Well, I never!" she exclaimed, and disappeared into the kitchen for the vacuum.

"Sometimes," sighed Duncan as he piled the lemonade mix and crackers into a carton, "Christmas isn't as much fun to prepare for as everyone says it is."

Fiona nodded sadly. "Right!" she said.

5

Mending fences

Blue Harbour was peaceful that night. The bright white new moon shone down on the still water of the cove, where the fishing boats rode at anchor. The two buoys—the bell and the groaner—broke the silence with their eerie sounds, and somewhere a dog barked for a moment and then was silent. It was cold after the thaw, and the smoke rose up in straight lines from the chimneys of the houses. Around the U-shaped harbour the fish stores shone starkly in the cool light, their wharves piled with lobster traps and coils of rope and large fish boxes. All the world seemed to be asleep.

But in at least two Blue Harbour houses, peace did not reign. At the MacDermids' house, Mrs. MacDermid tossed restlessly from side to side, and then finally got out of bed and went down to the kitchen to heat herself some milk.

As she stood there waiting for the milk to warm up she thought of Lorinda's face when she first saw the red vase, and then of what it looked like when she discovered that it

38

would cost thirty-five dollars. That small, thin face had registered excitement, bliss, shock and then despair, all within three minutes.

Then Mrs. MacDermid remembered the eager figures at the door yesterday, the card table, the bags, the supplies. She forced herself to recall her own short temper, her cross words, her exasperation and irritation. Regretfully she looked back on her own childhood, recalling another red-headed mother who was often angry.

As she drank her warm milk she forgot about her evening of vacuuming and washing, and thought instead of the abandoned little lemonade stand and the worried faces of her own children. "Tomorrow," she said to herself as she rinsed out her cup, "I will be a nicer person." Then she went upstairs and fell fast asleep.

Over at the Dauphinees', Lorinda lay on her back and stared at the ceiling of her room, watching the shifting lights as they shone in from the Government Wharf. She could not imagine feeling more sad. Yesterday's efforts had failed to make much money after expenses were taken out, and she had miserable memories of Reginald Corkum and his cruel taunts, of Mrs. MacDermid's anger, of worry and confusion and fury. Worst of all, she felt embarrassed and guilty because she had lost her own temper and gone stomping out of the store without so much as an apology or a thank you. How on *earth*, she asked herself, could I have done that?

Now, at three o'clock in the morning, she could realize that yesterday's experiment in the MacDermid store must have cost that family a whole lot of money in lost sales. She was old enough to know that it took a great many dollars to feed and clothe a family, and she knew that the gift shop was the MacDermids' only means of livelihood. She also knew that Mrs. MacDermid was a busy and often tired woman, doing three jobs at the same time—keeping house, being a mother, and looking after the store during Mr. Mac-Dermid's buying trips or when he was making craft articles in his workshop.

Lorinda winced when she thought of Mrs. MacDermid spending last evening cleaning up the mess that she and James had made. She jumped out of bed, being careful not to wake Jessie, who was making gurgling sounds in the crib by the window. "I'll make an I'm-sorry card," she whispered to herself, and picking up her crayons and construction paper from her desk, crept downstairs where she could work with a light on.

Half an hour later the card was complete. She had drawn a picture of a sad looking girl with huge tears rolling down her cheeks, and the words "I'm sorry" were spelled in four different colours across the top. Inside was the poem:

Mrs. MacDermid, I confess
We made a horrible, awful mess.
You think we are terrible kids, I guess.
Will you forgive us? Please say yes!

At four that morning Lorinda returned to bed and fell asleep immediately.

* * *

40

As soon as they returned from school the next day, Lorinda and James left their house and set off in the direction of MacDermid's Gift Shop. Lorinda carried her card, and James brought along a little cactus plant. He had been tending that cactus tenderly ever since August, and suddenly last week it had borne a lovely little pink flower. It was very hard for James to give it away, but every time he had tried to think of something that would be nice enough to make Mrs. MacDermid feel better, all he could think of was the cactus. So he clamped his teeth together hard, closed his eyes tight, and put it in a brown paper bag. He tried not to think about it as he and Lorinda walked around the harbour and past the Government Wharf towards the shop. He had often been told that you should give away gifts with a glad and giving heart. Well, I'm giving, he thought to himself, but I'm certainly not glad.

As they approached the gift shop, Lorinda and James started to walk more slowly. "I'm scared," said James, his eyes dark and worried behind his glasses.

"Fiddlesticks!" said Lorinda sharply. "There isn't a thing to worry about." But she discovered that she was shivering, although she had on her warmest clothes.

When they reached the store they stopped at the door and looked at one another.

"Oh, Lorinda," groaned James. "Do you think she'll still be as fierce as a tiger? I'm scared of you when you're mad, but she's much more scary."

James' fear suddenly made Lorinda feel almost brave.

"Anger can't hurt you," she said to him. "So stop worrying. It's not like lightning striking or being run over by a truck, you know. When we leave here, we'll still be in one piece, no matter *what* she does."

And then the door opened. There was Mrs. MacDermid, all smiles, asking them to come in, and actually saying that *she* was sorry. Lorinda and James were so surprised that James tripped over the threshold and fell flat on his face. The cactus went flying out of his hand and landed on the floor, paper bag and all, right side up.

"Oh, Mrs. MacDermid," he panted, rubbing his cheek as he rushed to pick up the plant, "I brought you a beautiful present. It's a cactus, and I've looked after it all by myself for four months. Look at it. Look at it! It's got a *flower*!"

When Mrs. MacDermid saw the plant, she did all the right things. She said that it was a gorgeous flower, that he had been wonderful to look after it so well for so long, that he had been terribly generous to give it up. James kept nodding all the time she was speaking, particularly at the point where Mrs. MacDermid said it had been very generous of him to part with it. Without even realizing what he was saying, he repeated, "*Very* generous."

Then Lorinda coughed slightly, and handed her card to Mrs. MacDermid. Mrs. MacDermid looked at it for a long time without speaking. When she did speak, her voice sounded soft and wobbly. "Thank you, Lorinda," she said, "for such a lovely card. You are a very good artist, and I'll treasure this forever. I'm going to put it up on my notice board in the kitchen, where it will remind me of you and of being sorry. Because I'm sorry too, Lorinda." Then she gave Lorinda a great big hug, and Lorinda found herself feeling that Mrs. MacDermid was one of the nicest people in Blue Harbour.

All the while this was going on, Fiona and Duncan were sitting on the stools behind the cash register, watching the whole scene. Duncan felt it was a good time to speak.

"Right you are, Mum!" he said. "She's a very good artist. And since they can't make money at a lemonade stand anymore, and since everyone seems to be so sorry about everything, this seems like a good time to tell you about our other idea—Glynis's idea, really."

There was a small silence. Mrs. MacDermid thought, Oh my heavens, what have they come up with *now*? Maybe I've carried that I'm-sorry thing a little too far. Aloud she said to Duncan, keeping her voice as calm and as friendly as possible, "And just what was that idea, Duncan?"

Duncan hopped off the stool and rushed over to join the group by the door. "Listen, Mummy," he cried, flinging his arms wide. "It's the greatest idea. And no mess. No cracker crumbs. No spilt lemonade. You'll *love* this idea!" His red hair stood up at the back of his head, giving him a surprised look.

Mrs. MacDermid tried again. "What idea, Duncan?"

"Lorinda wants to make hasty notes and sell them in our store. Isn't that great?" He was grinning broadly, and he looked as though he had just given his mother a beautiful present. In fact, everyone was smiling—Fiona, Duncan, Lorinda and James—everyone, that is, except Mrs. Mac-Dermid.

She fixed her eyes on the opposite wall and tried to do some fast thinking. What on earth do I do now? she thought. They're sorry, I'm sorry, and everyone is trying to be nice, including me. But much as I like Lorinda's card, and although I'll enjoy having it in my kitchen, how can I possibly put her hasty notes in my *store*? Mrs. MacDermid sat down on the nearest chair because she suddenly felt very tired. Problems, always problems, she thought. Nothing ever seems to be straightforward and simple. This is a very high class store. My customers expect to find the very best in here. If I put a pile of Lorinda's homemade cards on display, it's going to lower the tone of the whole shop.

Aloud she said to the children, smiling weakly, "I'm thinking." James and Lorinda were starting to feel nervous again. What had they done wrong this time?

Then Mrs. MacDermid looked at James' flowering cactus. She looked at Lorinda's I'm-sorry card. She looked at the four worried faces in front of her. She took a deep breath, and tried to smile.

"All right," she said. "You go off and make your hasty notes, and when you've made at least ten packages of them I'll put them on that corner table where I keep the paper napkins and notepaper. I'll make a little sign that says *Made by Blue Harbour Children*. Be sure you package them neatly," she added. "And don't forget to put in the right number of envelopes!"

Now it was Lorinda's turn to give Mrs. MacDermid a big hug. "Oh, thank you, Mrs. MacDermid!" she exclaimed. "You won't be sorry. I'll make absolutely beautiful hasty notes, and I'll have them ready for you before next weekend. I can do my homework real fast, and spend the rest of each day working on the cards. Don't you worry about a thing!"

Mrs. MacDermid smiled bravely and waved goodbye to Lorinda and James as they left the store. "Don't rush," she said. "I'm in no hurry."

Later that evening she said to her husband, "How could I have managed to get myself trapped twice in one week? There wasn't any possible way I could have said no."

Lorinda and James ran almost all the way to Coolen's Variety Store. They spent the rest of their remaining money and bought scratch pads and envelopes and coloured pencils. "We'll use Mummy's plastic wrap for packaging," said Lorinda. "She'll never miss it."

When they reached home they smuggled their packages into the house and hid them at the back of Lorinda's closet. She could hardly wait to start. Maybe they would make a whole lot of money after all. Surely nothing could go wrong this time.

6

Plan number two

That week was a busy one for Lorinda and James. They had to get up long before dawn to prepare for school, washing their faces and brushing their teeth in a bathroom that was still chilly, and then going down to eat their bacon and eggs in the kitchen, beside the warm stove that crackled and spat with its load of fresh logs. Then they rushed to pick up their books, and ran out to join the other children in the little group beside Hyson's Hill. The yellow bus took an hour to reach school and an hour to bring them home. Then came homework until suppertime, although Mrs. Dauphinee couldn't understand why Lorinda and James weren't using the lovely fresh snow for coasting.

''But you've been complaining about no snow ever since the thaw,'' she said, bewildered. ''It's only four o'clock. Why don't you go out? I like to see you having fun.'' But Lorinda would just mutter something about homework, and disappear upstairs with James.

One day when she and her mother were in the kitchen,

Jessie came trotting in, dragging a cart with the cat in it. "Secret! Secret! Secret!" she sang, and put one finger on her lips. Lorinda snatched her up off the floor and dashed upstairs to the bathroom—the only place where she could be sure they wouldn't be disturbed.

"Jessie!" she begged. "Please! Please! Stop saying that! Mummy will get suspicious."

"Okay," said Jessie. "Pretty vase. Red vase. Secret."

Lorinda sighed. "The date I really look forward to this year is December twenty-sixth, when I can stop worrying about what you're going to say." Then she picked up her sister and gave her a big hug. "I love you so much, Jessie," she whispered, and gave her a kiss on the end of her nose. "So be my friend, will you, and do what I say?"

Jessie threw her arms around Lorinda, speaking into her ear, "Pretty vase. Secret." Then she struggled free, and stood at attention before Lorinda. Putting both her hands over her mouth, she mumbled, "No say," and then raced off downstairs to rejoin her mother in the kitchen.

After supper there were more questions when Lorinda and James started back upstairs. "Surely you've finished your homework by now!" exclaimed their mother.

"Stick around," said their father, "and we'll have a game of Monopoly."

"Oh, gee, Daddy, we sort of have some stuff to do upstairs," said James, racing off after Lorinda. Mr. Dauphinee chuckled. "Do you know what, Alice?" he said to his wife. "I bet you're the only mother in Blue Harbour who nags her children not to do their homework.''

When James and Lorinda reached the top of the stairs, James poked his sister and pointed to the foot of the steps. There was Jessie standing on the hall mat, with both hands held over her mouth. "So far, so good," grinned Lorinda.

*   *   *

Each night James and Lorinda worked hard. Lorinda drew little scenes on the scratch pads—sailboats, fish stores, lighthouses, islands—and then coloured them. After that James folded them carefully and wrapped them in plastic wrap, with the scene showing on the smooth side. Lorinda signed each little picture *L.D.* and James put a slip of paper in each package, on which was written *Seaside Notes by Lorinda Dauphinee. $1.00*. There were ten notes in each package.

They worked very quickly and very hard, and by Friday night they had made up ten packages. Lorinda had been asked to make lunch and baby-sit at the Himmelmans' Saturday at noon, so they would have to deliver their cards to the gift shop in the morning.

Saturday morning was a dazzling day, with a bright December sun shining on a windy blue sea and on the sparkling snow. "Great day for coasting," said James, as he and Lorinda trudged through the snow to the Mac-Dermids' store.

"Yes," said Lorinda, "but not for us. We have to go straight from the MacDermids' to the Himmelmans', because it's going to take me all morning to get dinner ready while you play with Glynis to keep her from bothering Mr. Himmelman. Mrs. Himmelman said he'd be doing his law work in his study because he's got an important court case next week.''

James sighed. ''Sure would like to go coasting,'' he said.

''Oh, gosh,'' said Lorinda. ''Me too. And wouldn't it be awful to be grown up and have to work all the time? We'll be all finished on Christmas Day, but fathers and mothers have to keep on working forever. Just try to concentrate on Mummy and the vase. She's the best mother in Blue Harbour. She tells great stories, and she always wants us to be happy and healthy. She worries a lot, which is a pain, but she's almost never crabby. If she was crabby, I don't think I could stand all this work.''

''Like Reginald Corkum's mother,'' said James. ''She scolds him every time she opens her mouth, and you know what his father's like. Sometimes I almost feel sorry for him.''

''Well *I* don't,'' said Lorinda. ''If he'd try smiling for a change, or if he'd do something a little bit *kind* for the first time in his life, I might feel different.''

''I dunno,'' said James after a pause. ''I don't know one single kid who likes him very much, and that would be enough to make almost anyone act pretty ugly.''

''Which he does,'' said Lorinda, ending the discussion.

By now they had reached the MacDermids', and they were excited as they opened the door and heard the bell jingle. Mrs. MacDermid would be pleased with all the work they had done, and this time no one had anything to be cross about.

As soon as they were inside they could see that Mrs. MacDermid had a sign all ready on the corner table. It read *Handmade Hasty Notes by Blue Harbour Children*.

"Well, I'm a child, not a children," said Lorinda, stamping her feet to get the snow off, "but that sign sure looks good all the same. Here!" she announced, handing the bag of notes to Mrs. MacDermid as she came in from the back of the store.

Mrs. MacDermid took the notes out of the bag and looked at them. She did not speak and she did not smile. They were even worse than she had feared. The drawings were simply and roughly drawn, and some of the colours weren't even between the lines. "I guess you did these pretty quickly," she said, looking up from them, a line between her brows.

"Yes," said Lorinda, stiffly. "We did a hundred."

A hundred! thought Mrs. MacDermid bleakly. Why didn't she do ten and do them properly? Well, I can't tell her they're nice, because they're awful. But I can try to smile.

Oh, dear, thought Lorinda, who suddenly realized how tired she was.

Mrs. MacDermid took a deep breath and managed a cold, weak smile. "Thank you, Lorinda. Put them over there by the sign."

Lorinda could feel all the morning's excitement and pride seeping out of her, like the tide going out and leaving the sand damp and cold. She walked slowly over to the table and arranged the cards in two little fanlike groups of five. Then she went to the door and said, "Thank you, Mrs. MacDermid," and opened the door.

"Oh, and Lorinda," said Mrs. MacDermid as they prepared to leave, "don't make any more. I'm sure this will be quite enough. Good morning, dear. Have a nice day."

"A nice day!" mumbled Lorinda as they set off for the Himmelmans'. "James, she didn't say one single nice thing about all our work. She didn't even mention the packaging!"

James tugged Lorinda's sleeve. "*I* thought they were beautiful," he said. "Maybe she didn't say anything because she couldn't think of anything nice enough to say. She probably loved them."

Lorinda came upon a pop can in the middle of the road, and kicked it so hard she sent it flying across the road and right onto Mr. Morash's wharf.

"Don't be silly!" she snapped. "She did *not* love them. She *hated* them. You always think people are thinking nice things, James, but I know better. She doesn't want any more. Didn't you hear that? So even if we sell them all, we'll only get ten dollars, and don't forget we've already spent over five dollars on supplies. Do you know where that will get us? Right back where we started. Oh, good grief! Look who's coming!"

And there was Reginald Corkum walking along the road from the direction of the wharf.

"Oho!" he cried. "If it isn't the Dauphinees! How is the

great red vase, the ugliest vase in Blue Harbour? Bought it for your mother yet?''

Lorinda looked straight ahead of her as she passed him. ''Not yet,'' she replied, ''but soon.'' To herself she thought, I think I'll be sick all over the road if I have to look him in the eye.

But they were almost at the Himmelmans', and Lorinda did not often hang onto her gloom for very long. If they could not make money at the MacDermids', they would make it at the Himmelmans'.

7

Plan number three

By the time Lorinda and James reached the Himmelmans',
they were both feeling cheerful again. James' job was to
keep Glynis busy so that Mr. Himmelman could do his
paperwork in peace. But keeping Glynis busy wasn't really
work. She was two years younger than James, but they
were good friends, and they both liked to do the same sorts
of things. They loved pretending they were people they
weren't, and liked playing Pirates, or Store, or Hospital, or
Detective. Glynis had a puppet theatre and some puppets,
and they made up long, complicated plays and took the
parts of all the characters. Sometimes they just liked to sit
and draw, or even just talk.

Lorinda was starting to feel pleased about her day too. In
the kitchen she found a menu, and a list of all the ingredi-
ents she would need. She was to prepare hamburgers and
baked potatoes and frozen peas, and for dessert there
would be the last of Mr. Himmelman's birthday cake. In the
freezer was chocolate ice cream, in case anyone wanted it

with the cake. George was out coasting with Duncan and wouldn't be home until half past twelve, so she had the kitchen all to herself.

While James was in the living room playing with Glynis, Lorinda started her work in the kitchen. She chopped up the onions, beat two eggs and stirred in the hamburger meat. Then she added pepper and celery salt and shaped it all into patties. She washed the potatoes and turned the oven on and got the peas out of the freezer.

How lovely to be making money doing anything this easy, she marvelled, as she started to set the table. She decided she would serve dinner at twelve-thirty sharp.

Lorinda didn't want to keep Mr. Himmelman waiting for his dinner for even two seconds, so she had the hamburgers cooked and the peas boiled and ready by twelve, and set them at the back of the stove to keep warm. At twelve-fifteen she looked at the peas and saw that they were all wrinkled, like the faces of old men.

By twelve-thirty Lorinda was no longer feeling peaceful and pleased. George had not yet arrived home. The hamburgers were starting to look dry and tired, and the peas looked puckered, like fingers that have been in water too long.

Just then Mr. Himmelman appeared, asking for his dinner. He was tall and sandy-haired and handsome, and also very hungry. Running her fingers through her long black hair and shuffling nervously, Lorinda asked him if he could wait awhile longer, until George turned up.

54

Then she caught sight of something at the back of the stove. The potatoes! She had forgotten to put them in the oven. Quickly she popped them in, her heart sinking fast. Any dumb bunny, she told herself, knows that potatoes take an hour to bake. She sat down on the kitchen stool and fidgeted. She didn't know whether to be mad at George because he was late, or to wish he would stay away long enough for the potatoes to bake. She didn't know what to think about anything anymore.

"If only I wasn't so tired," she sighed. Glynis's cat, Cleopatra, was meowing, and she didn't know where to find the cat food. The peas were looking worse and worse, and the hamburger patties were starting to look like hard black mud pies. As she brought the jug of milk out to the table she tripped over Cleopatra, spilling milk across the tablecloth and onto some of the cutlery. Muttering to herself, "Oh dear, oh dear, oh dear, oh dear," Lorinda raced back and forth between the kitchen and the dining room, changing the tablecloth, pitching the milky cutlery into the sink, resetting the table. At one o'clock Mr. Himmelman appeared again.

"Do you suppose I could eat now," he asked, "even if George isn't home yet? I'm really starved. Are you okay, Lorinda? You look sort of red and hot and bothered."

"I'm just fine, Mr. Himmelman," said Lorinda, "*just fine*. And I'll bring your dinner right away."

Mr. Himmelman sat down at the table, and then stood right up again.

"Oh, my heavens!" cried Lorinda. "You've sat right on the soaking wet tablecloth. Are you all right? I mean, are you very *wet*?"

Mr. Himmelman, always a very polite man, sat down carefully. "Don't give it a thought, Lorinda," he said, wriggling around a bit on his chair. "A little wetness never killed anybody. And these are jeans I've got on; they can go right into the tub."

Relieved but rattled, Lorinda served his dinner. She put a large spoonful of wrinkled peas on his plate, added two black hamburger patties, and finally served the potato. It was so hard that it actually went *klunk* as it hit the plate.

Mr. Himmelman started at the noise, but didn't say anything for a moment. Then, as she turned to go back to the kitchen, he asked, "May I please have the buns for the hamburgers?"

Lorinda did not scream or cry or rush from the house. She just sat down on one of the dining-room chairs and put her head in her hands.

"Mr. Himmelman," she said through her fingers, "the buns are still in the freezer and hard as rocks."

Mr. Himmelman looked at the forlorn figure before him, and then at his plate again. "That's all right, Lorinda," he said. "The meal looks delicious just as it is. Let's skip the buns today, eh?" He picked up his knife to cut into his potato. Lorinda fled to the kitchen so that she wouldn't have to see him struggle with it.

At least the birthday cake looked good. She cut Mr. Himmelman a huge piece, piled three scoops of ice cream on top of it, and took it in to him. Then she brought in his coffee. After that she went out to the kitchen and stood all by herself in the pantry, biting her nails. Before long she heard the scraping of Mr. Himmelman's chair against the floor and heard him call out, "Thank you, Lorinda, for the great dinner! I really enjoyed that a lot."

Alone in the pantry, Lorinda decided that sometimes it must be okay to lie, if the lies were as kind as Mr. Himmelman's.

At one-thirty George came strolling in, saying cheerfully, "Gee, I'm sorry, Lorinda. Just forgot all about the time."

Lorinda gave him a furious look and said, "Go and get Glynis and James. They must be almost *dead* with hunger." Then she served the shrivelled little peas and the dried-up meat and the perfectly lovely baked potatoes onto their four plates. She wished she could take a potato up to Mr. Himmelman's study so he could see how well she really did bake them.

George was not as polite about the meal as Mr. Himmelman had been. He complained about the lack of buns, asked for ketchup and mustard, remarked about the funny looking peas, and gave her a lecture on how to serve meat that wasn't all dried up and overdone. Lorinda was so mad that when she came in to take away his plate she snatched it too quickly and knocked a glass off the table and broke it. As she swept up the broken glass George made her feel even worse by saying, "That's one of our best glasses. It's part of a set. We only use them at Christmas and Thanksgiving."

Lorinda's heart was like a stone inside her chest. She put the food away and swept the floor and washed the dishes, but she was so weary and sad and discouraged that she could hardly manage to finish. She wished she could crawl into a nice comfortable bed and pull up the covers and sleep for a whole week. She wished that Christmas were in August. She wished she were a millionaire. Most of all she wished she hadn't broken that glass. Next time she wouldn't do anything wrong at all.

But there was to be no next time. When Mrs. Himmelman returned from Halifax she thanked Lorinda warmly for all her work, and praised her for leaving the kitchen so lovely and clean. Then she said that her Aunt Hattie had been released from the hospital that very day and had gone back to her home in Digby.

"What's more," Mrs. Himmelman added, "I got all my shopping polished off and I won't have to go into Halifax again before Christmas. Isn't that wonderful? I'm really grateful to you and James, Lorinda, for helping me out so well on this last day." And she gave Lorinda her pay for the work that she and James had done.

"So that's that!" declared Lorinda as she and James walked from the Himmelmans' to the variety store. "There goes nothing!"

"I thought it was a really nice day," said James.

Lorinda didn't even bother to comment. She was too tired to feel annoyed. When they reached the variety store she crossed both sets of fingers on both hands and asked

Mr. Coolen, "Do you have a drinking glass called 'Etched Rose' in your store?"

"Well, yes, as a matter of fact we do," he replied. "Usually we don't carry crystal, but we keep a few of those on hand because it's the Himmelmans' special set."

Lorinda uncrossed her fingers and discovered that she could breathe again. "How much for one glass?" she asked.

When Mr. Coolen told her the price Lorinda had to sit down on one of his packing boxes. She took out her wallet and gave him the money, taking the glass from him without even looking at it.

As they left the store and started for home, Lorinda spoke to James. "Do you realize," she said, "that the glass I broke cost exactly five cents more than the money we earned today? And do you know something else?"

"No," said James. "What?"

"We can't do it. It can't be done. We've worked for over a week and we're five cents behind instead of thirty-five dollars plus tax ahead. It's as though that vase didn't *want* to belong to Mummy. If we worked for thirty years we couldn't ever make enough money to buy it."

James stopped walking and stared at Lorinda. "You mean we're going to *give up*?" His eyes were shocked and miserable.

"That's exactly what I mean," replied Lorinda, all the spark and energy gone from her voice. "I'm going to see Mrs. MacDermid tomorrow and tell her to pitch those hasty notes into the sea. It's obviously what she'd like to do with them anyway.''

"You don't really mean that, do you, Lorinda?'' gasped James.

"No,'' said Lorinda, "of course I don't. But tomorrow we'd better go over there and see if we can find some dumb present that we can buy for a couple of dollars, just in case Mrs. MacDermid sells two packages of those awful old notes. We might be able to buy . . . an apron.''

"Or maybe we could give her ten packages of hasty notes,'' said James.

"Oh, James!'' said Lorinda. "That's not very funny.'' Then she managed a sad little chuckle. "Do you know what I did, James?''

"What?''

"I put salt into Mr. Himmelman's coffee instead of sugar. They keep their salt in a little bowl beside the stove. The cup was empty when I cleared the table, but Mr. Himmelman didn't even say one single thing!''

"But he couldn't have drunk it, Lorinda! He takes two spoonfuls in every cup. What do you think he did with it?''

"I think it's a mystery,'' said Lorinda.

8

Success at last

The day looks just exactly how I feel, said Lorinda to herself as she sat up in bed and looked out the window. All the bright, sparkling snow was gone again, and the winter rain was coming down in a straight, dismal line. Everything was grey and wet—the sky, the sea, the wharves, the cliffs. Streams of slushy water were pouring down Hyson's Hill and over the road, and you could tell that it was cold and raw just by watching the way people were walking, all hunched over with their heads down.

Lorinda sighed and climbed slowly out of bed. This is the day, she thought, when James and I go over to the Mac-Dermids' and pick out an awful present instead of a perfect one. We haven't got one single solitary cent left, but surely someone will buy at least one or maybe even two packages of notes. All we have is a box full of a million completely useless scratch pads.

She discovered that she was talking out loud, even though she was all alone except for Jessie, who was asleep.

Suddenly Jessie sat up in her crib just as Lorinda was saying, "And what's more, we'll have to walk all the way over there in the pouring rain just to say that we can't buy that vase."

Jessie stood up and put both hands over her mouth. "Secret," she mumbled through her fingers. "No say."

"Oh, Jessie," cried Lorinda, "you've been so good. Not," she added sadly, "that it's done us any good."

Two hours later James and Lorinda were slopping along the road on their way to the MacDermids'. The rain was coming down even harder, and the boats at anchor in the harbour were getting more and more full of water. Neither Lorinda nor James spoke. There didn't seem to be anything to say except sad things, so no one talked. Every once in a while one of them would sigh, and they walked slowly, as though they were on their way to a funeral.

But at last they reached the MacDermids', their clothes soaked and their hair hanging limp and sodden against their faces. James could hardly see a thing out of his wet glasses.

"Oh, gosh, James," groaned Lorinda, "we're wet again. Mrs. MacDermid won't like that any better than she likes my hasty notes. Give yourself a good shake before you go in."

But the door opened before they could do any shaking, and in the doorway stood Mrs. MacDermid, her red hair brightening the grey day and a big smile all over her freckled face.

"Come in! Come in!" she cried, spreading her arms

wide. "You're just in time for hot cocoa to warm you up." Lorinda looked at James and James looked at Lorinda. Here was another mystery.

When the children stepped into the store they could see Fiona and Duncan behind Mrs. MacDermid, actually jumping up and down, their smiles broad and excited and their freckles shining in the bright overhead light. A big pitcher of steaming cocoa stood on the counter, and there was a plate of blub-blubs beside it. Blub-blubs were chocolate-covered marshmallow cookies, James' favourite.

"We were just about to phone you," said Mrs. Mac-Dermid. "We thought you should know right away, because today's Sunday and you'll have some free time."

"Should know *what* right away?" asked Lorinda, more and more puzzled. "And who needs free time? And for what?"

Mrs. MacDermid raised her right arm and pointed dramatically to the table in the corner. "Look!" she exclaimed. "Gone! Every one!"

Lorinda and James didn't know what she was talking about for a moment, but then they understood. The hasty notes had disappeared from the table. All that was left was the sign saying *Handmade Hasty Notes by Blue Harbour Children*. Beside it was a smaller sign saying *Temporarily out of stock*.

Lorinda didn't speak for a minute. During the past two weeks she had jumped so often from happy to sad to happy to sad and back again, that she wanted to be sure of what had happened before she allowed herself to be happy.

"You mean people bought them? *All* of them?" she asked, stunned.

"Not only that!" announced Mrs. MacDermid. "They *loved* them! Customers kept saying how charming they were."

"And we're going to need a whole lot more!" Fiona broke in.

"And two women actually had a fight over who was going to get the last set!" cried Duncan, rubbing his hands together.

"Lorinda and James," said Mrs. MacDermid, "I'm so happy for you. And for me too, because several of the women said they would be back next week, bringing friends. So, look. Drink your cocoa, and go right home and start working. You have a whole free day, and I'll bet you can make me several sets by the time you go to bed. James might like to try making some too. You can drop them off tomorrow on the way to the bus stop. And you can make more after school next week. And here," she paused, flourishing the money, "is your ten dollars."

James had been hugging himself with pleasure ever since he had seen the empty table. But it was only now that Lorinda let herself be excited. She threw her wet self at Mrs. MacDermid and gave her a hug, and then sat down with Fiona and Duncan and James to have cocoa and blub-blubs.

While they ate, George and Glynis came into the store to

64

buy some gift-wrap. When they heard the story they were as thrilled as the others.

"Look, Lorinda," said George, "Glynis says I was pretty awful yesterday about your terrible meal." Lorinda closed her eyes. "And it was sad about you breaking that really expensive glass and all." Lorinda winced. "So," he continued, "I'd sort of like to help you. How be Glynis and I do the packaging and labelling? If we wrap for you, James and you can spend your whole time drawing. You can come over and work in our basement playroom, and then your mum won't have any idea what you're doing."

"And we can be your advertisers!" cried Duncan, pounding his fists together and pacing up and down. "When people come in the store, we'll just happen to mention how nice the notes are."

"And Lorinda," said Mrs. MacDermid, "just put five cards in each package. We'll sell them for fifty cents, and that way we can keep more people happy. Some of our customers were really angry when we ran out of them yesterday."

"Well!" said Lorinda, standing up and returning her mug to the counter. "We can't just sit around here and be sociable. Let's go!"

So they left. Lorinda and James went to the variety store for new packages of plastic wrap and Scotch tape, and then stopped off at their own house to pick up their drawing materials. By ten-thirty they were hard at work in the Himmelmans' basement.

That day and the coming weeks were even busier than the previous seven days had been. But it was a lovely way to work hard. Mrs. MacDermid sold their cards as fast as they could make them, and each evening Lorinda and James counted their money and put it away in a shoe box at the bottom of Lorinda's closet. They were coming very close to having enough money for the vase.

But it was James who finally brought their money up to thirty-five dollars plus tax and beyond it. On the following weekend, tired of drawing, he went out and washed Mr. Morash's truck for him, charging him fifty cents. He did such a good job that before long there were cars lined up beside the Dauphinee barn, honking for service. He worked all weekend, and by Sunday night the shoe box was actually heavy.

At eight o'clock that night, Lorinda and James carefully closed the door of Lorinda's room and counted the money. Forty-six dollars and fifty cents! They counted it twice, because it was hard to believe. But it was true. They had earned forty-six dollars and fifty cents, and at last they could go over to the MacDermids' and buy that vase, giving their mother the most beautiful Christmas gift that she had ever had in her entire life.

They both thought they would be too excited to sleep, but they had forgotten how hard they had worked and how tired they were. In the morning Lorinda slept right through the alarm, and had to be wakened by Mr. Dauphinee. They were so late they almost missed the school bus.

66

They got to the bus stop just as the last child got on. By the time the Dauphinees were in, there were only two seats left, one at the back and one at the front. James went to the back of the bus and took that seat, and Lorinda sat down at the front without noticing who was beside her. When she finally looked and saw Reginald Corkum, she nearly fainted. She would far sooner have stood up for the whole thirty-kilometre drive than sit beside him. As she said to James later, "I felt *polluted.*"

But it was too late now. He leered at her and taunted, "Well, well, well! If it isn't old Lorinda Dauphinee, the big money-maker. Made enough to buy that disgusting red vase yet? Or is your rich father going to give you the money?"

Lorinda could hardly wait to answer. She actually didn't feel one bit mad, even when he put in that part about her rich father.

"Well, yes, Reginald," she said, speaking slowly, "as a matter of fact we *have* made enough money for that perfectly beautiful vase. In fact, we made *more* money than we needed. And what's more, we're going over there tomorrow evening after supper and we're going to pay Mrs. MacDermid thirty-five dollars plus tax and we're going to take that heavenly vase home with us. We'd go tonight if we didn't have to baby-sit Jessie. On Christmas Day my mother is going to be so happy that she probably won't even be able to taste the turkey."

Reginald just looked at her. He didn't say one word.

Then he turned his head and looked out the window. He stayed like that for the whole thirty kilometres. Lorinda almost enjoyed the ride.

Then, as they arrived at school, Reginald pushed past her into the aisle, and spun around. Sticking out his tongue he cried, "I hope she hates it. I hope it breaks. I hope you lose the money. I hope it's all counterfeit. I hope the vase has a big, fat, furry spider in the bottom of it. So *there*!" His eyes were wet, and Lorinda watched in amazement as a single big tear rolled down his face.

She stood, shocked, in the centre of the aisle, but as she remembered his words she started to feel cold with fury. Then James was pulling on her sleeve. "Never mind, Lorinda," he said. "He's just mad because everyone likes you and no one likes him. Don't pay any attention to him."

Lorinda took a deep, quavery breath. "Oh, James," she sighed, "you're probably right. But he sure knows how to scrape the frosting off a cake."

9

A shock

The next morning Lorinda woke early and watched the moon set over the dark water, thinking to herself that it had never looked more beautiful. She felt like a fairy princess lounging on her canopy bed, warm and secure under a coverlet of woven gold. She felt like a millionaire who had nothing more important to do than to pass the day deciding how to spend her money. She felt like a mountain climber who, after spending three weeks clawing her way up the rock face, had finally reached the top. She felt like Lorinda Dauphinee who had had a dream and was watching it turn into the real thing.

She was a strange mixture of peaceful and excited. One part of me, she thought, feels like lying in bed all day and just thinking about how happy I am to be me. Another part of me doesn't know how I can *live* through all those hours of breakfast and bus and school and lunch and homework and chores and supper before James and I can go over to the MacDermids' to pick up the vase.

But the day finally did pass. Supper was over, and at six James and Lorinda put on their hats and coats and boots and mittens, and yelled a goodbye to their parents.

"Just going over to the MacDermids' on an errand!" they shouted as they opened the back door.

"Okay," called their mother from the kitchen, and their father added, "But come back right away. And be careful on the road. It's dark."

They almost ran to MacDermid's Store. When they opened the door Lorinda felt as though there should be bugles blowing or a drum beating. There should be something more triumphant than that tinkly little bell to announce their arrival. But there were Mrs. MacDermid and Fiona and Duncan in the shop, vacuuming the floor and dusting the shelves and counters.

"We're here!" announced Lorinda, giving the bell an extra shake to celebrate. Nothing was wrong this time. Mrs. MacDermid was full of smiles. There was no slush to mess up the welcome mat. No cracker crumbs spoiled their entrance. And best of all, Lorinda's pocket was bulging with money.

"We have come," and she paused dramatically, raising her right hand for silence, "...for the *vase*!" James just stood there, smiling and smiling.

Then there was great excitement for a few minutes. Mrs. MacDermid stopped the vacuum and rushed over to shake their hands and congratulate them. Fiona and Duncan dropped their dusters and danced a jig right in the middle of the store.

Then Mrs. MacDermid said, "Well! I guess you don't want to just stand there and wait any longer. We'll get the vase right now, and Fiona will gift-wrap it for you." She went off to the office to bring it out of its hiding place.

"Now I guess she's not so cross about having to hide it away for us," whispered Lorinda. "As Mummy would say, 'Thirty-five dollars plus tax will buy a lot of lettuce.' "

Mrs. MacDermid had been humming a little tune when she left the store to go into the office. Then the humming stopped, and there was a long silence. "Oh, gee!" said Lorinda to James. "I wish she'd hurry. It seems years since I've seen it."

"Fiona! Duncan!" Mrs. MacDermid called from the office. "Come here!" James thought her voice had that special knotted sound that parents' voices sometimes have when something awful is happening that they want to keep secret.

But Lorinda didn't notice. She was still hugging herself and hopping from one foot to the other.

James was no longer smiling, however. He was biting his thumbnail, and there was a line between his eyebrows.

When Mrs. MacDermid and Duncan and Fiona returned, even Lorinda could see that something was terribly wrong.

"Lorinda. James," Mrs. MacDermid began. "Look. I don't understand. I really don't. It was there yesterday afternoon. I saw it when I went to get some staples. There must be some very simple explanation."

"You don't mean to tell me," Lorinda interrupted in a voice that was so quiet it was almost a whisper, "that the vase is. . .*gone*?"

"Yes, Lorinda, it's gone. But I'm sure there's nothing to worry about," Mrs. MacDermid said, looking as though she was going to drop dead of worry in the next five minutes. But before she could say any more, Mr. Mac-Dermid came in the back door of the store, whistling a Christmas carol and carrying a pile of miniature lobster traps that he had been making in his workshop. He stopped whistling when he saw everyone.

"Hey!" he exclaimed, "What a sight! Why all the long faces? Don't you know that Christmas is coming?"

Lorinda shut her eyes. "Don't I know Christmas is coming!" she said out loud. "Oh boy! Do I ever know it!" Mr. MacDermid was perhaps the kindest, most good-natured, friendliest man in Blue Harbour, but Lorinda found herself feeling angry at him for being able to whistle at a time like this. And for being so cheerful.

"Angus," said Mrs. MacDermid, "do you know anything about what happened to that red vase that was in the cupboard in the office?"

"Sure!" said Mr. MacDermid triumphantly. "I sold it! Thirty-five dollars straight into the cash register. Plus tax. That should buy a couple of turkeys!" He chuckled.

Suddenly they were all speaking at once. Didn't he know they were saving the vase for Lorinda and James? No, he didn't. Well, *why* didn't he know? Because no one had told him. What on earth did he think they were setting up lemonade stands and making hasty notes and washing cars *for*? Well, he had heard it was so they could buy a present for their mother, but no one had ever told him exactly what present. How on earth did he know it was there, wrapped in the brown paper bag and shoved to the back of the cupboard?

"Because I was told that it was there," replied Mr. MacDermid.

"By whom?" demanded Mrs. MacDermid.

Fiona's fist flew to her mouth, and all that showed of her face were two frightened eyes.

"By Reginald Corkum," answered Mr. MacDermid.

Lorinda sat down on a chair, and her face was very white. "And then what?" she managed to ask.

"He said it was in there because it had been set aside," said Mr. MacDermid. "I assumed he meant set aside for *him*. I didn't ask. Then he bought it. He said it was for his mother. Fiona wasn't around, so I gift-wrapped it myself, because it seemed like such a generous gift for a boy to buy for his mum." Mr. MacDermid scratched his bald head. "I don't understand any of this. How did he know it was there?"

Fiona was crying and didn't answer. Lorinda spoke instead.

"He's known it was there right from the beginning," she said, her voice flat and sad and colourless. "What's more, he knew exactly why it was there. It wasn't a generous gift, Mr. MacDermid. It was probably the most *cruel* gift you ever sold. I think I will wear black for the rest of my life. I think that if I live to be a hundred-and-ten years old, I will never again live through a Christmas Day as awful as it's going to be this year at our house. I want to lie right down in the middle of your shop and die six times, one after the other." And Lorinda leaned her back against the door and closed her eyes.

Mr. MacDermid, of course, felt terrible. It wasn't his fault, but he felt so miserable that he had to sit down too, with his little lobster traps all piled in his lap.

"Lorinda and James," he began, "I can't even half begin to tell you how sad and sorry I am. I wish I could press a button or wave a magic wand and make that vase come back. But I can't. The best I can do is phone the potter and ask if he has any more vases like it in stock, or if he can make another. But we all know," he said, sighing and shaking his round head, "that Christmas is right around the corner. And I feel I have to tell you that I just don't see how all this can be done in time. But we'll try." He rose from his chair and dumped all the lobster traps on a table. "Right now." And he set off for the office to use the telephone.

"Mrs. MacDermid," sighed Lorinda, putting her arm around James' shoulder, "I don't think I can stand waiting around for any more bad news. If something nice happens, let me know. Otherwise I don't want to hear anything at all. I just hope for Reginald Corkum's sake that I don't meet him on the way home." And she opened the door, the bell jingled, and they were gone.

"Sorry, James," said Lorinda as they walked toward home, "but I can't even pretend to be cheerful or hopeful or anything. Maybe tomorrow, but not tonight. I'm just going to devote the whole evening to being depressed." James nodded.

In the distance they could see Reginald Corkum watching them from the far end of the Government Wharf. He didn't shout or laugh or tease or come near. Perhaps he didn't dare. And he looked sort of small and sad and bedraggled, as though he wasn't even getting any pleasure out of what he had done.

10

The longest week

One short week remained before Christmas. The holidays had started, and when Lorinda woke up the next morning it was already light, the day bright and sunny. Beyond the harbour the bay was full of whitecaps that sped out to sea on an offshore wind. Lorinda could see Mr. Morash's boat coming into the harbour with his morning's catch. "Full, I suppose," she said to herself when she saw how low the boat was riding in the water. "But who cares? There could be five million haddock in that boat and it wouldn't matter to me."

"The day has no business being so beautiful," she muttered as she slowly dressed. "It should be black and raining, with a raging wind. Instead, it looks like a postcard or a picture in a book. And all those beautiful gulls are sailing around the sky when they should be on my mother's red vase."

Downstairs the phone rang—two long and one short—and her mother called up the stairs, "For you, Lorinda."

It was Mr. MacDermid. He told Lorinda not to get her hopes up too high, but that the potter had sent an identical vase to another gift shop. *If* he could locate it, and *if* it had not been sold, and *if* it could be sent to Blue Harbour in time for Christmas Eve, then all would be well. But those were a lot of ifs. Nevertheless, from where she stood at the telephone, Lorinda found that now she could bear to look out the window at the beautiful day. She wasn't really very excited, but at least she could say to herself, "Well, maybe, just maybe." She found herself smiling into the receiver.

"Thank you very much, Mr. MacDermid," she said, and hung up. Then she went upstairs and told the news to James. He just looked very solemn and said, "You know what, Lorinda? I'm tired of expecting that things are going to be good and then finding out they're not. I'm going to try hard not to think."

"Good idea," said Lorinda.

But try as she might, Lorinda found it impossible not to think. She even started feeling hopeful and cheerful again, but this time with a sad little piece of fear mixed in, spoiling the fun of it all. She could watch herself getting cranky about the least little thing, and Mr. Dauphinee remarked to his wife, "Lorinda blows up if you so much as look at her sideways."

She called the MacDermids' so often that Mrs. Mac-Dermid started feeling a bit edgy too. "Listen, Lorinda," she said, trying to sound patient, "you *know* the mail only comes once a day. There's no point in calling four times.''

It was certainly not an easy week to live through. The members of the Postal Union were threatening to go on strike, and Lorinda and James knew that if the mails closed down, all hope would be lost. Lorinda found herself watching the TV bulletins as eagerly as her father, hoping for news of the strike vote.

"I really don't understand," said Mrs. Dauphinee as her husband came into the kitchen to make a cup of coffee. "Today I actually saw her turn off a cartoon and switch to the CBC news. She watched so eagerly you would have thought her life depended on it. When I came in to ask if she wanted a peanut butter sandwich, she yelled, '*Quiet*, Mummy! I missed what he said!' I just don't understand at all.''

But the threatened mail strike was not the only problem. Four days before Christmas a ferocious winter storm hit Nova Scotia. Sixty centimetres of snow came down and blew into impassable drifts, and for twenty-four hours no one could use the roads. Mrs. Harrison had her baby at home because she couldn't reach the hospital, and a whole shipment of turkeys was two days late in reaching the variety store. Telephone lines were down in some places, and for a while Lorinda couldn't even phone the Mac-Dermids. It wouldn't have mattered anyway, because only a dog team could have brought the vase to the Mac-Dermids' that day. The mail drivers were all sitting home playing crib, rejoicing about the big storm and enjoying their first holiday since summertime.

But the biggest crisis of all came when Lorinda lost the money. The day before Christmas Eve, just to cheer herself up a little, she went into her closet to count the money in the shoe box. She turned on the closet light, sat down on the floor on top of her running shoes and skates and old toys, and opened the shoe box. It was empty.

"No!" cried Lorinda. "This can't happen to me! It just *can't*!" At that moment James came in and she told him what was wrong.

"Of course it's not there," said James. "You took it all out that day we went over to buy the vase."

"Oh, my gosh!" gasped Lorinda. "So I did. I must be losing my memory. I put it in the pocket of that old ski jacket I was wearing. You know, in the big zipper pocket."

"Lorinda!" James grabbed her arm so hard it hurt. "I heard Mummy say yesterday that she was going to send that jacket to the dry cleaners, and then I saw her dump it in the clothes basket."

Lorinda flew out of her closet and down the hall to the bathroom. She dove into the laundry basket and there, on the very bottom, found the jacket with the fortune in its pocket. Lorinda took out the money with shaking hands and transferred it to the shoe box.

"James," she said, "I'm going into my room to lie down and stare at the ceiling. If anything else awful happens today, don't tell me about it. For instance," she said as the phone rang in the kitchen, "if that's Mr. MacDermid saying that they absolutely can't get the vase, please don't tell me. I feel like I might just possibly blow up and burst if I hear any more bad news. Tomorrow's Christmas Eve, and I don't even dare *think* about it.''

Her mother called out, "It's for you, Lorinda!" and then muttered to her husband, "Why do you suppose Mr. Mac-Dermid keeps calling Lorinda?"

When Lorinda was through with the phone call she went over to her mother and gave her a huge hug. Then she kissed her father, hugged the cat, and grabbed James' hand and dragged him upstairs.

"What *now*?" exclaimed Mrs. Dauphinee. "I love her to pieces, of course, but she certainly is a very odd child sometimes.''

"Jessie!" cried Mr. Dauphinee suddenly. "What on earth's the matter?"

Jessie was standing in the middle of the kitchen with both hands over her mouth. "Secret!" she was mumbling.

Upstairs, Lorinda put her hands on James' shoulders and stared at him hard.

"What?" demanded James.

Lorinda shut her eyes.

"It's arrived," she said very softly. "It came. It's really and truly there!''

* * *

Within ten minutes James and Lorinda had eaten a quick breakfast and were in the back porch getting ready to leave.

80

"Hey, Mummy!" called out Lorinda, "we're going over to MacDermid's Shop for a while."

Mrs. Dauphinee came out to the porch and watched them as they put on their outdoor clothes. "That's fine," she said. "Have a good time; but try not to get in their way too much. Tomorrow is Christmas Eve, and they'll probably have a whole lot of customers in the shop." Then she paused. "It's such a lovely store," she said wistfully, "with so many beautiful things in it."

"Red vase!" said Jessie suddenly, right out loud, and Lorinda's heart skipped at least four beats.

"*Jessie!*" roared Lorinda.

Mrs. Dauphinee bent down beside Jessie. "What was that you said, dear?" she asked. But Jessie was standing with both hands over her mouth.

"Why does she keep doing that?" mused Mr. Dauphinee from over by the fireplace where he was mending his nets.

Mrs. Dauphinee reached up to get James' hat off the hook. "Oh," she sighed, "I wish I could go with you to see all the MacDermids' Christmas stuff. Maybe Jessie and I could go too."

Lorinda stood very still and held her breath.

"No. I can't," continued Mrs. Dauphinee, and Lorinda started breathing again. "I have the hard sauce to make and some other secret things to do. But I'll bet their Christmas merchandise is gorgeous this year. I haven't been in for two weeks, and they always bring in some really special things at the last minute. Mind you," she chuckled, "they sometimes have some terrible things for sale, too."

"Like aprons," agreed Lorinda.

"Well," said Mrs. Dauphinee, "I wasn't thinking about aprons. I remember seeing something in there way back in October that was really awful. It wasn't there the last time I was in, so someone must actually have bought it. If you can imagine!"

"What was that, Mum?" asked James as he struggled with his boots.

"Maybe you didn't see it," said Mrs. Dauphinee, bending down to help him, "although if you did, you'd certainly never forget it. It was an ugly red vase that had a lot of sea gulls flying all over it. Hideous! And very expensive. My word! It's hard to believe that anyone would take it for nothing, let alone spend good money on it. But the world is full of strange people!"

She straightened up from helping James with his boots. "There now! You're all ready!" she said. "Why are you just standing there? Off with you! Be sure to come back in lots of time for lunch. Do you have your heaviest mitts on? It's cold. And Lorinda, you look a bit pale. I don't want you getting sick before Christmas." She turned and went back to the kitchen, humming happily to herself.

11

The gift

Outside the Dauphinee back porch, Lorinda and James stood in the deep snow and just looked at one another.

"Well!" sighed James. "What now?"

Lorinda was so stunned that her head felt like a whirling top. She tried hard to think, but her thoughts all came out backwards and upside down and tangled together and spinning around.

"What now?" she repeated. "James, I have no idea what now. The best idea I can think of right now is for us to go to sleep in some quiet hole somewhere and wake up on Boxing Day."

"Aw, c'mon, Lorinda," said James, taking her hand. "Don't be sad. Let's go for a walk. A beach is a nice place to be when your life is a big mess."

Lorinda was always the one who was looking after him, but suddenly he could see that Lorinda needed a lot of looking after herself. He pulled her hand and hauled her across the path and down the road to the little beach overlooking Pony Island. Where the tide had gone down, there were frozen jellyfish and frosty pebbles and empty shells. They walked up and down for a while and even tried playing tag with the waves, but Lorinda didn't seem to feel much better. Her shoulders were hunched, and she walked as though she were a hundred years old.

"Hi!" It was Glynis, all bundled up in her red snow suit, with a navy blue hat that came down over her ears. Her blonde pigtails were shining in the early morning sunshine. "Why do you look so sad?" she asked. "Fiona told me the vase came. I thought you'd be jumping over the moon."

So they tried to explain. "Everything was wrong and then suddenly everything was perfect, and now everything's a great big nothing," said Lorinda.

Then James told Glynis about what had happened in the back porch—how they had discovered that their mother had seen the vase and thought it was *ugly*. And Lorinda explained about how she was so disappointed and confused that she couldn't even think.

Glynis's face got sadder and sadder as she listened. "Lookit," she said. "If you really can't think up any new ideas, I can fix everything. I gotta go now and do an errand for Mummy, but I tell you what I'll do. I'll lend you my Thinking Rock on Elbow Beach. You can have it for one whole day." She paused. "And that's all you'll need," she added.

When she was gone, Lorinda was frowning. "*Her* Thinking Rock!" she snapped. "Does she really think it's hers to lend? Rocks don't *belong* to people—not the ones on public beaches anyway. Silly kid stuff. I can do my thinking standing up, thank you."

"Aw, Lorinda," begged James, "just try it. And everyone calls that big rock 'Glynis's Thinking Rock.' Gee whiz, she's on top of it half the time. And she sure is full of a lot of good ideas. It was nice of her to lend it, even if it isn't exactly her own rock. C'mon, Lorinda." He yanked at her coat sleeve again. "Elbow Beach is a really neat place anyway. Let's go and just *try*."

Lorinda was too tired to argue. She thought to herself, James is bossing me around, and I don't even care. If he suggested that we walk to Halifax today I'd probably go. They started off around Spruce Point by the shore path, and over to Elbow Beach. There, just at the point where the two sides of the beach met, was the Thinking Rock. It was about three metres high, but there were grooves and depressions in it so that it was easy to climb even when it was slippery.

"Go on!" urged James. "I bet when you get on top of that thing you'll know right off the bat what we should do."

"James!" cried Lorinda. "It's Christmas Eve tomorrow! I can't! It's too late."

"It's *not*!" snapped James. Lorinda had not known he was capable of snapping. "If Glynis, who is only five, can think of good ideas on that rock, just imagine what you can think of! You're ten. Don't be such a chicken!"

That did it. Lorinda was halfway up the rock, ice and all,

before the next wave rolled in. On top was a round depression where a person could sit, and Lorinda sat down and looked out to sea.

From here she could see the horizon ("All the way to Spain," her father often said), and the sky was enormous, with no trees in the way. Just looking at it made Lorinda's mind feel big and open and wide and free and empty. She let it be empty for a while, and sat and watched the gulls diving for fish, the red bell buoy rocking back and forth, the whitecaps rushing over to Spain. She listened to the waves, like rolling drums, down by the tide line. She shut her eyes and felt the wind on her face. I'm ready, she suddenly thought, to start thinking. My insides are all peaceful again.

"James," she said aloud, raising her arm, "I'm starting. Don't talk or whistle or anything. Just wait."

James smiled to himself. He was good at waiting. He could never see why people got impatient waiting, or why they found it boring. If there was nothing to watch or listen to—and there usually was—you could always go inside your brain and spend the time in there. "Take as long as you want!" he called up.

I know what I'll do, thought Lorinda. I'll have a conversation with myself. With two sets of ideas, maybe something will happen. And she started her conversation.

What would Mummy really like for Christmas?

I don't know.

Why don't you know?

Because she's not here to ask.

Well, you couldn't ask her anyway, because presents have to be secrets.

But it should be something she wants. We sure found that out this morning.

Okay, then. What does she like?

Oh, all sorts of things. Pretty clothes, jewellery, pink nighties.

Does she have lots of those things? No point in getting her something she's got already.

No. She doesn't have much at all. She's always looking in store windows in Halifax and sighing.

Why doesn't she have lots of clothes and jewellery?

Silly! You know why. Because we're poor. She doesn't have enough money.

"*Money!*" yelled Lorinda, and stood up so fast that she nearly fell off the rock. "That's *it!*"

"What's it?" asked James from the bottom of the rock, where he was sliding his fingers over the slippery back of a jellyfish.

"That's what we'll give her!" cried Lorinda as she climbed down off the rock. "The money! The whole forty-six dollars and fifty cents. She never has anything to spend for the January sales, and I've often heard her say it's sad that at the one time of year when things are cheap, no one has any money to spend. Not *us*, anyway."

James stood up and gave Lorinda one of his biggest smiles. "That's a real good idea, Lorinda!" Then he couldn't resist saying, "I guess that old rock isn't so useless after all."

"Useless!" huffed Lorinda. "I wish I could write my school exams up there. I bet I could get a hundred in all of them, even if I didn't know anything." Then she whirled round and round on the slippery sand. "Oh, James!" she cried, "this is ten times better than the vase! This way she'll get exactly what she wants, and it'll probably be the biggest surprise she ever had in her whole life! Whose mother ever looked into an envelope and found forty-six whole dollars and fifty cents?"

"You know, that rock works even when you're standing at the bottom of it," said James. "I just thought of an idea too. Besides, an envelope isn't a very exciting *looking* present, even if what's inside is wonderful."

"Okay. What, then?"

"We could go to the variety store," said James, "and buy some coloured construction paper and put it in a loose-leaf binder."

"So?" said Lorinda. "Who wants a book full of coloured paper?"

"Just wait," said James patiently. "You sound like Reginald Corkum."

Lorinda clenched her fists and shut her eyes.

James continued. "We'll have to take some of the money to buy these things, but that's okay—there's lots left. Next we ask Mr. Coolen to change the money into one-dollar bills, and then we tape a dollar on every page. When it's all done, we wrap the book up in the most beautiful paper we can find at MacDermid's Shop. And wow! *A Money Book*! What a gift!'' James grinned, and then added, ''Mummy won't forget this Christmas till she's an old, old lady.''

''And, oh boy,'' laughed Lorinda, ''neither will we!''

12

The day arrives

And certainly no one in the Dauphinee family did forget that Christmas. The children rose early, while it was still dark, but later on the sun shone down on the village, brightening the white snow to a dazzling brilliance.

James and Lorinda had spent so much time and so much worry over their mother's present during the past six weeks that they had almost forgotten about the presents they would be getting themselves. They looked at the stockings hanging from the fireplace as though they had never seen them before. Even though their back porch did need mending, and even though Mr. and Mrs. Dauphinee wore the same few sets of clothes month after month and year after year, and even though the bills for Mr. Dauphinee's cough medicine seemed to get higher and higher, the Dauphinee Christmases were always wonderful; and as Lorinda said to James, "Every year there seem to be lots and lots of presents."

This year the stockings bulged with marshmallow

brooms and magic markers and puzzle books and bubble gum. And Jessie even found a Raggedy Ann doll underneath the tree. Mrs. Dauphinee had made it in the evenings when Jessie had been asleep, and it had black button eyes, red wool hair and even an embroidered heart. Mr. Dauphinee had made James a bookcase for his books, and had painted it bright red to match the curtains in his bedroom. Lorinda got a pair of figure skates—her first—with long white boots and picks on the front. She hugged them to her chest and sighed.

"Now I won't have to wear Cousin Henry's old black hand-me-downs anymore," she said, "and with the picks I can learn how to do all those turns and twirls."

Mrs. Dauphinee got a beautiful amethyst ring from Mr. Dauphinee, and she had made him a warm wool cable-knit sweater. With Lorinda's red mittens and scarf, he looked very handsome in the navy blue pullover. And James had made him ten complimentary car wash tickets for keeping his truck clean all winter long.

Lorinda had asked that their gift for Mrs. Dauphinee be opened last. Although she and James were excited, they were also ready to wait. There was so much to do and watch and enjoy. The tree was beautiful. They had strung rows and rows of rosehips, and the red chains circled the tree over and over again. Wonderful turkey smells floated in from the kitchen, and signs of Christmas were every-where—the bright red tablecloth, the centrepiece that Mrs. Dauphinee had made, the little dishes of jellybeans and gumdrops that seemed to be on all the tables, and the boughs of spruce and fir that Mr. Dauphinee had hung over the pictures and between the banisters on the hall stairs. And through it all was the delicious thought that Mrs. Dauphinee would soon be opening their present. It was a bit like reading a really good book. You didn't want the story to be finished, but you were dying to know how it would end.

And James and Lorinda were not disappointed. When Mrs. Dauphinee opened the gift she was so amazed, so thrilled, she couldn't speak for almost a minute. She just sat there and turned page after page, while her mouth and her eyes opened wider and wider. Then she kept saying, "I don't believe it! I just don't believe it!" over and over again. And when Jessie started dancing around, singing, "No secret! No secret! No vase!" James and Lorinda told the whole long story, from the time Lorinda had first seen the vase until they had made up the book on Christmas Eve.

It was a fun story to tell—about Reginald Corkum, the lemonade stand, the hasty notes, the overdone hamburgers, the car wash, and about trying to keep Jessie quiet for almost four long weeks. As they told the story, Mrs. Dauphinee's eyes started to look shiny and wet, and James was sure he saw one lone tear slide down her cheek and onto the book. (Later on he checked, and the ink *was* a little bit blurred on that page.) And she was so pleased that when she gave them their thank-you hugs, Lorinda thought she was never going to let them go. Then Mrs. Dauphinee rose and sort of floated out to the kitchen, where she began rattling dishes and blowing her nose.

The day was as close to being perfect as a day can be. In the afternoon the Himmelmans and the MacDermids came over to have some Christmas cake, and all of them were able to add pieces to the story. Everyone there—except Mr. and Mrs. Dauphinee—knew about the struggles to earn money for the gift, and each person was able to tell his or her own version. The talk was full of remember-whens.

"Remember when the lady in the mink coat spilled lemonade down her front?" Mrs. MacDermid was able to laugh about this now.

"Remember when you broke the glass?" said George. Lorinda still didn't find that too funny.

"Remember when everyone bought the hasty notes in *one day*?" That was certainly easy to remember.

"And, oh, Mr. Himmelman. Do you remember the wrinkled peas?" Yes, he sort of did, but it had been a great meal anyway. "And what did you do with your salted coffee?" Mr. Himmelman just smiled.

"Aw, c'mon, Mr. Himmelman," begged Lorinda. "We've been trying to figure it out ever since."

"Well," he said, "if you really want to know, I poured it over the pot of geraniums. They've been blooming extra well ever since."

Soon afterwards the MacDermids and the Himmelmans left, and Mrs. Dauphinee bustled out to the kitchen to test the vegetables. Then the turkey came sizzling out of the pan and the family sat down at the red table. Candles were lit, and they shone on the browned potatoes, the dish of squash, and the bowl of Solomon Gundy, made especially for Christmas with the herring caught by Mr. Dauphinee and with onions from their garden. And of course the turkey, gleaming and steaming and golden on the platter, was the best part. It was even more delicious than the mince pies or the hard sauce.

Finally Mr. Dauphinee lit a fire in the Franklin stove, and everyone grouped around the old family pump organ to sing carols. Lorinda felt as though this day was so perfect, so happy, that it would be able to keep her warm through every single cold and difficult day that might lie ahead for her.

At last it was time for bed, and there were many thank-yous and hugs and kisses under the mistletoe.

Later in the evening Lorinda and James crept down the stairs to watch the grown-ups, and they could see Mrs. Dauphinee leafing through the catalogue. They watched while she stopped to admire a page full of expensive dressing gowns, and then some beautiful nighties, and finally a page full of jewellery. They heard her say, "Oh, Jim! I'm going to have about three months of fun just trying to make up my mind before I finally decide what to spend that money on."

Then Lorinda and James started slowly back upstairs. Near the top, Lorinda suddenly stopped, and spoke in a surprised voice. "Do you know what, James?" she asked, turning to him. "The Christmas spirit must really be digging me in the ribs pretty hard. I just caught myself hoping that Reginald Corkum's mother really and truly likes that vase!"

"Me too," said James. "That's really weird."

They sat down on the top stair and listened to the carols coming from the record player.

Lorinda sighed. "I love it so much," she said. "Christmas, I mean. Just listen, James." From below they could hear:

Peace on earth and mercy mild,
God and sinners reconciled.

James looked at Lorinda out of the corner of his eye and bit his thumb nail.

"Lookit, Lorinda," he said finally, staring hard at his bedroom slippers, "you're not going to like this idea, but I just had a thought."

"Oh, oh!" said Lorinda. "What now? It makes me nervous when you get thoughts. Better get it off your chest."

"Well," he began, "next month's your birthday. I sort of wondered if maybe you could. . . ." His voice trailed off.

"Oh, no!" exclaimed Lorinda, very firmly. "Not *that*! Reginald Corkum is *not* going to get himself invited to my birthday party. Not then. Not ever."

"But we pretty much know he's mean because he thinks no one likes him."

"Not *thinks*. *Knows* no one likes him. And he's right. They don't."

"But maybe"—James bit off a whole slice of thumb nail and looked at it, frowning—"just *maybe* if you pretended to like him enough to ask him to your party, he might try to be different. He *might*, Lorinda."

"No!" she said.

James sat and thought for a moment. Then he smiled a slow, crafty smile. "Lorinda," he said, "it would please Mummy and Daddy a whole lot if you did. It really made them sad to see him standing out in the cold last year. Nose running and all. Slapping his hands to keep them warm."

Lorinda sat very still and said nothing.

From downstairs they could hear the record coming to an end:

When peace shall over all the earth
Its ancient splendours fling,
And the whole world give back the song
Which now the angels sing.

And then there was a silence.

James looked at Lorinda. Lorinda looked at James. He had the good sense to say absolutely nothing.

Lorinda sighed—a big, long, groaning sigh. "Oh, gee, James," she said. "Okay, I'll do it. For Mummy and Daddy. For Christmas. And because that doggone carol has me feeling all squishy inside."

"Oh, Lorinda!" James reached across and hugged her so hard she grunted out loud. "Let's call it your first New

Year's Resolution," he said, as he let her go.

"Right you are," she replied as they rose from the step. "New Year's Resolution Number One, and the hardest one I ever made." She grinned. "Wow!" she breathed. "*What a day!*"

"Right *you* are!" said James.

And then they went to bed.